Also in this series

DAVID ROSS AND BOB CATTELL

CARLTON

A catalogue record for this book is available from the British
Library.

1 3 5 7 9 10 8 6 4 2

ISBN: 978-1-84732-548-8

Printed in the UK by CPI Mackays, Chatham, ME5 8TD

Bob Cattell was born in the Fens and now lives in Suffolk.
He combines his job as a copywriter with writing children's
books about football and cricket – including the Glory
Gardens series. He is a lifelong Aston Villa supporter.

David Ross was somehow always the reserve in his school
football team, which gave him lots of time to observe the
game. He loves to hate supporting Heart of Midlothian
and has written numerous other books for children.

1
THE BIG EASY

Nicknames are very important for any football team, and Sherwood Strikers was no exception.

At Strikers most of the players received theirs from Dean Oldie who had a rare talent for finding the perfect name. In fact, some believe that Deano even came up with his own nickname. 'Psycho' described him perfectly – he was a complete mental case. Over the years he had picked up a number of other names too: 'Jaws' because of his serious shortage of teeth, and 'Red', probably because of the number of red cards he got.

Most of the other players in the Strikers team owed their nicknames to Psycho. Cosimo Lagattello's love of Italian food and his well-reported weight problem earned him the title 'Pasta', whilst his Strikers colleague in the Italian national team got the name 'Eetsa' Gambolini because every single sentence he spoke in English began 'Eetsa': 'Eetsa beauti-ful game', 'Eetsa not a right' and so on. Dave Franchi was known as 'Superglue'; Brad Trainor, 'Perky'; Ashleigh Coltrane, 'Slow Trane' and skipper Jamie MacLachlan and Lanny McEwan were, of course, 'Big Mac' and 'Little Mac'. Drew Stilton hated being called 'Cheesy' but that just made Deano use the name all the more.

The two young stars of the England World Cup triumph, Jason Le Braz and Thomas Headley, had somehow not really picked up a nickname in their first season with Strikers although Thomas was sometimes known as 'Deadly' to rhyme with his surname. However, on their return to Sherwood for pre-season training Deano was ready and waiting for the pair of them. Jason was unkindly christened 'Ferret' for his speed down the right wing – Deano said he'd just renamed his son's ferret 'Braz' as a sort of double compliment – and Thomas? Thomas earned the name 'DD' or 'Didi' which Psycho said came from his two goals in the World Cup final against Holland – DD stood for Double Dutch.

After all the excitement of England's World Cup triumph, it was business as usual at Sherwood

Strikers. The entire squad was on a pre-season tour for some light training in New Orleans where, since their arrival, temperatures had soared into the upper 30s and training had become very light indeed. Mostly it consisted of a couple of lengths of the hotel swimming pool – what Dave Franchi called, 'getting in training for a good day's slob'. They had two friendlies against American opposition during the trip, the first against Houston Harriers, whom they'd beaten 2–0 earlier in the week, and the next day's game against the New Orleans Dixies. But mostly it was a chance for the players to relax before the new season got properly under way with the Charity Shield at Wembley against Highfield Rovers in ten days' time.

The big news at Strikers had been manager Joss Morecombe's signing of French star, Paul Claudel from St James, for £25 million. Claudel had played a major part in getting St James into the European Champions League the season before although, because he'd fallen out with the manager of the French national side, he hadn't played in the World Cup. Thomas Headley, for one, was looking forward to playing alongside the French forward whom he rated as one of the world's greats – on his day probably the greatest. But Claudel had the reputation of being a strange character and a difficult man to manage. Would he fit into the Strikers set-up? Or would there be a clash of personality with other temperamental characters such as Pasta Lagattello and Cheesy Stilton? Only time would tell.

The other close season signings had both been in midfield: Austrian Petr Pahler, who already had built up a big reputation playing in Germany, and Franco Jordan, a 19 year old who had scored a lot of goals for First Division Cowbridge Athletic. Len Dallal, the Strikers' assistant coach, reckoned Franco was the best value of the three. 'He's a real worker,' said Len with enthusiasm. 'The lad puts himself about, plays with his heart. I like players who do that.' The implication was that he thought the manager had paid far too much for Claudel – and a lot of other people thought so too, particularly the press.

Len Dallal – known to the players as Doolally – was the only notable absentee on the New Orleans tour. Doolally hated flying. He'd been in an aeroplane only once and there was nothing Joss Morecombe or anyone else could do to get him to fly across the Atlantic. So training sessions for the time being were in the hands of Len's assistant, Warren Fitzroy, and Strikers' speed-strength-and-diet guru, Doc Martin.

4

The other news was that midfield utility player, Paul Bosch, was on the transfer list and there were rumours too that England star, Dave Franchi, was also looking for a move. The loss of Dave from the Strikers' back four would be a big blow, but it was no secret that he wanted to captain a Premier League side and both White Hart United and Border Town were jostling to sign him as player-manager. It was clearly only a matter of time before he moved on, although Dean Oldie made his views about it pretty clear.

'You're out of your box, Superglue,' he said. 'Stay and win the league with us. If I play against you I'll probably have to break your leg for being a traitor to the Reds. And I wouldn't want to do that, would I?'

'You'd do it for fun,' said Dave with a smile. 'Listen, Psycho, I know Sherwood's a great side. But even you can't stay here forever, mate.'

'I can't blame you selling out while you're still worth something. But that doesn't mean I have to like it. I've got used to playing alongside the ugli-est face in football,' said Dean.

'Look in the mirror sometime, Psycho,' said Dave with a laugh as he wandered off for another swim.

'I love the thin red line
They may be ugly
But they're all mine.'

Deano grinned his six-teeth smile as he happily sang one of the Strikers fans' favourite songs about the legendary back four of Oldie, Franchi, Trainor and El Harra. Since Ben El Harra's injury at the back end of last season Jason Le Braz had come into the reckoning. Now with Dave leaving it seemed like the end of an era.

Apart from the heat, another reason for the light training was the fact that Doc Martin, the club's diet and fitness guru, had scarcely been sighted on the tour so far. After organising the early morning running sessions and diet sheets he would disappear from the team's hotel for the rest of the day. Rumours that he was sightseeing or frequenting the bars of downtown New Orleans were finally laid to rest when he turned up late one afternoon with a lanky American in a tracksuit and baseball cap, whom he introduced to the players as PeeWee Wannamaker.

'PeeWee's coach of the New Orleans Bays,' said Doc enthusiastically. 'He's got a lot of new ideas about fitness and team interaction which I'd like to give a try.'

'Pleased to meet ya'all, drawled PeeWee. 'As I guess you all know, the Bays is one of the top football teams over here. That's football, American football, not soccer, of course. The Doc here says you're all a great bunch of guys and I'd be pleased to pass on a few of my ideas to some Great Brits. I guess the big one that we're all excited about at the Bays right now is what we call Clanship. It's a fancy name and a big idea – and we think it gets results, hey Doc?'

'It's brilliant" enthused Doc. The Strikers' players had learned a lot from the Doc since he'd joined them the previous season. The little rubber ball of a man had developed a speed and fitness programme at Strikers which had given the Reds the edge over many of their opponents in the last quarter of the game. A high proportion of their goals had been scored in the last ten or 15 minutes because they were outrunning other teams. Doc's boldest innovation was an individual swipe card which registered how much time each player spent on each piece of gym equipment. So everything you did in training could be monitored daily. But the Doc had been known to get carried away with his own modernising enthusiasms and Len Dallal in particular was highly suspicious of his methods. It took all Joss

Morecombe's tact and diplomacy to maintain the balance between Doolally, the traditionalist, and Doc, with his new ideas. For instance, towards the end of last season, Doc had tried to persuade the boss to hire a full-time aromatherapy and reflexology healer whom he rated as his spiritual mentor. Rosie Shakespeare was her name; she was about 103 with orange skin and red hair and eyes that were full of madness. Joss tactfully allowed her to give him a foot massage, pronounced it wonderful, but then came in the next day limping. He told the Doc that he didn't dare risk Rosie on the feet of multi-million pound footballers. The Doc had been out-played and he knew it.

But PeeWee was another matter. His methods had been tried and tested on one of America's top NFL teams. The American football writers worshipped him and rightly, so Doc said. His results were said to be astonishing, shattering, ground breaking. 'It's all about testing everything – diet, exercise, sleeping hours, training – and getting yourself into synergy with the players you interact with.'

'Pardon me, ya'all?' said Deano in an American drawl.

PeeWee smiled feebly. 'For instance, we each

have our own mantras at the Bays,' he said casually.

'Mantras?'

'It's like a chant. The quarter-back and centres, say, get together twice a day and chant their mantra – like getting into each others' heads. Then they have their own training programme, and they eat together – the same food and—'

'It builds up a telepathy,' said Doc with a bright gleam in his eyes which made his glasses sparkle.

'Let me show you a video,' said PeeWee. 'I think you'll agree after that that we have one impressive idea here which will work for you soccer players just as well as it does for our football players. Remember Clanship, hey, guys?'

The last thing the video produced was clanship or agreement. Predictably Dean Oldie, Dave Franchi, Sean Pincher and the skipper, Big Mac, thought it was a load of old mumbo jumbo. But Clanship had its supporters. The American, Brad Trainor, and Petr Pahler were really impressed with PeeWee's methods. Thomas Headley's best friends, Jason Le Braz and the US goalkeeper, Rory Betts, seemed prepared to give it a chance, too. As for Thomas, he wasn't sure – the video looked good but he wasn't really very keen on some of the chanting stuff. As Psycho said, the fans back at Strikers did all the chanting he wanted to hear.

PeeWee said his goodbyes, shaking hands with everyone in the team, and left them to argue about what they'd seen. 'Football's an instinct game,' said Rory. 'Reaction, form, timing: they all come and go – and no one knows exactly why. Maybe this will keep us better focused, more concentrated.'

'Constipated, more like,' scoffed Psycho.

'Aye, tha skinny lang smout's nae aydeah aboot fitba' playin',' said Big Mac. 'There's naught we'll lairn frae chantin' a wee silly toon.' Some of the players nodded in agreement though, as usual, scarcely any of them understood a word Big Mac said.

'Well I for one am sure with you, Doc,' said Perky Trainor. 'I guess there are a few of us who'd like to give it a try.' About half the squad mumbled in agreement.

'Good. Then I'll talk to the boss,' said Doc. 'Monty's already met PeeWee, and I know he's really impressed.'

The club chairman, Monty Windsor, was travelling with them on the tour, though the players only ever saw him at the large and generous lunches given by their American hosts.

The game against the New Orleans Dixies was no more than a light work out for the Reds. No one played for more than 45 minutes on account of the searing heat. Joss began with what he considered to be his first team selection at the end of the previous season and Drew Stilton scored within the first ten minutes.

Then after half an hour the boss experimented with Paul Claudel and Haile Reifer up front and by half time the Frenchman had scored a hat trick. Thomas was impressed with his astonishing ball control and ability to slip his marker and then slide past the oncoming defender with perfect poise and balance. He remembered something Joss had told him once: 'A defender only has to touch the ball once and he wins. A good striker needs speed, control, strength and belief in himself. A great striker needs all that and a bit of the thief and a bit of the magician.' Claudel was a great striker, no doubt about that.

The Italian pairing of Pasta Lagattello and Eetsa Gambolini was getting better and better too. Sergio Gambolini seemed a yard faster than he had been the season before and showed signs of linking up well with Claudel, too.

In the second half Petr Pahler replaced Big Mac and he too continued to look a strong, uncompromising player with good touch and plenty of skills. As Thomas came off to be replaced by Franco Jordan, he began to realise that the boss could well find himself spoilt for choice in his future selections. Although he had been one of the England heroes of the World Cup, Thomas knew that there were no guaranteed places in the Strikers line-up this season. Such was the talent of the side that every player would have to work hard to stay in the team and the competition for places would be at its most intense in midfield.

Strikers ran out 6-2 winners against the Dixies and, as their American tour came to an end, a new season beckoned for Sherwood. It seemed full of hope and challenge. As FA Cup winners their first game would be against the title-holders, Highfield Rovers, in the Charity Shield. That would be the first real test of their mettle and would shape the side for the first Premier League game.

Perhaps this year, for the first time under Joss Morecornbe's managership, Sherwood Strikers would bring home the league title. Sherwood was such a big club that Joss would be judged a failure if they were not battling to win the league at the end of the season. And he knew, if he failed this year, he was out. Success was the only thing Sherwood Strikers understood.

Squad numbers for the new season

Goal

1	Sean Pincher
20	Rory Betts
26	Ben Stockley

Defence

2	Dave Franchi
3	Brad Trainor

4	Jason Le Braz
5	Dean Oldie
14	Tarquin Kelly
16	Brian Robinson
19	Ezal Delmonty
25	Ben El Harra

Midfield

6	Jamie MacLachlan (captain)
7	Thomas Headley
8	Cosimo Lagattello
10	Sergio Gambolini
17	Paul Bosch (sweeper/midfield)
18	Curtis Cropper (midfield/striker)
21	Francisco Panto-Gomes
27	Petr Pahler
28	Franco Jordan

Forwards

9	Ashleigh Coltrane
11	Drew Stilton
12	Haile Reifer
15	Boris Poniowski
22	Paul Claudel
23	Aaron Bjorn Rorschach
24	Lanny McEwan

2

BACK TO REALITY

As the Jumbo broke through the clouds over Manchester, Thomas saw that it was raining. Back to training in the cold and sliding around in the mud, he thought grimly. He stretched and flexed his large frame – even in first class he could never get comfortable on a plane. Psycho and Sean Pincher were snoring noisily but Thomas never got a wink of sleep when he was flying.

The US tour had been just what he'd needed; he'd enjoyed the warmth of both the American hospitality and the climate. After the World Cup, he had felt completely drained. Now he was ready again, keen to start a new season. There was no more punishing league in the world than the English Premier League and the Strikers' fixture list was terrifying to behold. There was scarcely a week without two games until Christmas – starting with the Charity Shield at Wembley against Highfield.

Apart from the new signings there had been plenty of other changes at Strikers over the summer. The practice ground facilities had been completely redesigned, with a new gym, dressing room, baths and a brand new player's lounge with luxurious seating and wifi access. The Trent Park ground had new seating, too, and there was a brand new supporters' restaurant and a lot more building still going on. Things were happening at Strikers; there was a feeling of energy and expectation in the air.

The players' however, were less interested in their surroundings and much more concerned about the manager's ideas on selection. The line-up for the Charity Shield game was the big talking point. When Joss finally made up his mind, Thomas was relieved to see his own name featured in midfield. He knew that the rotation of players would be important if Strikers were going to build up a winning momentum in the Premier League, but he still wanted to play in every game. Like everyone else, his greatest nightmare was sitting week after week on the subs bench or, worse still, playing for the Reserves.

This was the team:

Reserves: Ben Stockley (goal), Jason Le Braz, Sergio Gambolini, Petr Pahler, Franco Jordan, Lanny McEwan.

Joss Morecombe was fielding a cautious mix of old and new talent, with the emphasis on defence. Sean Pincher was out with a throat infection which gave Rory a chance to star in goal. Jason was disappointed not to make the starting line-up but not as disappointed as Drew Stilton who wasn't even on the bench. Back at Wembley again after only a few weeks, Thomas felt he was walking on air. After the FA Cup final and the World Cup, some people might have found the Charity Shield a bit of an anti-climax, but not Thomas. He loved playing at Wembley, whatever the occasion. And a pre-season struggle against Highfield Rovers and his England friends and team-mates Graham Deek and Freddy Dade was the biggest stage as far as he was concerned.

From the opening minutes of the game things didn't seem to go quite right for Strikers, however. Highfield's loose 4–3–3 formation was much more adventurous than Strikers' rather defensive 4–5–1. Deck' Dade and Barry, operating in the gap between the Sherwood midfield and the flat back four defence, seemed to be able to run through at random.

After ten minutes Rovers were ahead. A little touch on by Dade was picked up by Mattie Barry and Deekie ran on to the perfect pass to slam the ball with his left foot past a static Rory Betts. It was a beautiful goal. The Highfield supporters roared their appreciation and the visiting Strikers fans held their breath for a moment before bellowing back:

'We'll take you to the cleaners in the end!'

Highfield's new multi-million pound sponsors' Kleen-Quik, had not only got their name emblazoned in gold on the team shirts but they seemed to have taken most of the advertising boards around the ground.

> 'O Clau-del, oh la la
> Give 'em hell, oh la la!'

The Strikers fans were in better form than the players this afternoon. But Claudel's first appearance in a red shirt wasn't turning out to be his greatest hour. Playing inside Thomas, the Frenchman's frustration over his lack of service grew and grew, and when he did get possession he wasted it with over-tricky runs or wild passes into space which no one read. He seemed to be playing on a different planet from the rest of the team.

'My ideas – they are are beautiful. They fly and you sit on the perches like fat pigeons,' he complained. Thomas half understood and half sympathised.

At half time Joss brought on Little Mac McEwan and Franco Jordan for Cisco Panto-Gomes and Claudel. The Reds began to show a bit more aggression and fight up front and Thomas soon realised that Franco had big potential. He was a tall, muscular player with a lot of raw talent and plenty of strength on the ball. A run on goal almost brought him a dream strike early on but his shot was half blocked and went wide. Strikers had more and more possession but they couldn't find a way through the Rovers' defence and finally the Highfield and England captain. Jimmy Stinger, found Dade on the wing with a brilliant long ball and the cross behind the back four was neatly met by Deek's diving header. The ball buried itself in the net behind a diving Rory Betts.

Strikers battled on. Little Mac came close with a glancing header. Big Mac had the ball in the net but Franco Jordan was ruled offside. And so the scoreline remained 2–0 until the final whistle.

Thomas Headley felt fairly philosophical about the game. He had played neither well nor badly. He had had little chance to influence play going forward and had been forced to tackle back to get possession. Highfield were a class act, the league champions, and it was no disgrace to go down to an organised side like them. But if Sherwood Strikers were going to win the title' they had to match Rovers' organisation and flair. Thomas took his little brother Richie's teasing after the game in good part. Richie was Highfield Rovers' number one fan and was now enrolled in Rovers' junior school of excellence and doing really well. He was beginning to grow fast, and it looked as though he might end up even taller, and rather slimmer' than Thomas, with pace to match. Any win by Highfield Rovers was an occasion for him to crow about' but victory over Sherwood was the best of all.

'All the money in the world won't win Strikers the league title,' taunted Richie. 'Claudel's rubbish and Jordan's not worth much either.'

'Wait and see, little brother,' said Thomas calmly. 'The new lads haven't settled down yet.'

'New look stadium, new look team, and where does it get you? Beaten by the best, again. I don't understand why Joss Morecombe didn't try to buy Dade or Deek rather than than that flash Frenchman.'

'There's nothing flash about Paul, he's brilliant. You wait until you meet him – you'll like him a lot.'

'He might be a nice Frenchman, but he's still flash on the football field. And how is it that Pahler's worth so much and he doesn't even get a game?'

'Plenty of time – it's a long season. And we'll be up there at the end. You'll see.'

*

Even Richie would not have predicted that Strikers, with their prestigious new signings, would go on to lose their first two league matches and draw the third.

Sherwood Strikers 1 – St James 3
West Thames Wanderers 1 – Sherwood Strikers 0
Sherwood Strikers 1 – Weirdale Harriers 1

One solitary point from three games; a dismal start to the season and one that no one, least of all the manager, was able to explain. The games were close enough and hard fought and they should have beaten the Wanderers – a Franco Jordan goal was disallowed on a very dubious offside decision, and Ashleigh Coltrane, normally the safest of penalty takers, fired over the bar from the spot. But the three late goals scored by St James were all down to lack of concentration and organisation at the back, and that wasn't like the Strikers back four. The press was full of theories – World Cup fatigue, over-confidence, poor preparation – but no one really had an answer.

To make matters worse the Dave Franchi transfer to Border Town finally went through and he became player-manager of his new club. Paul Bosch went with him in a double deal worth £6 million to Strikers. The club's shares soared on the back of this news and a hugely successful pre-season marketing campaign. No club had more fans worldwide and no organisation was slicker and more professional at bringing in the money. Strikers FC was a major industry of that there was no doubt. But everybody knew, not least the chairman, Monty Windsor, that this huge business empire depended ultimately on the results achieved by 11 players on the pitch. The club's shares wouldn't stay high if they didn't win their games. If Strikers weren't up in the top two or three, the shareholders felt it where it hurt, in their pockets. And if they hurt' they made sure that old Monty hurt with them.

But, in spite of the chairman's moans, Joss Morecombe remained unflustered as ever. He knew it would take time to get the best combination up front from Claudel, Coltrane, Stilton and McEwan. And he also had to work out how to integrate the undoubted talents of Franco Jordan and Panto-Gomes into a strong midfield where Headley Lagattello, Gambolini and the skipper, Jamie MacLachlan, were already well established. Too much choice was his problem – and he didn't mind that.

Coming up fast was Strikers' first game in Europe. They had been drawn against Galatasaray, the Turkish side, with the first leg away in the hot-house atmosphere of Istanbul. It was a key game. All of England would be watching and frankly Strikers needed a lengthy run on the European stage. After such a dismal set of early season results, this was a match that Sherwood had to win. The pressure was building.

3
CLANSHIP

'Strictly Private' read the notice on the door of the manager's office – his den he called it, and it was unquestionably more of a den than an office, the sort of den that an untidy collector of old cardboard boxes, worn-out armchairs and assorted rubbish would call paradise. This was the nerve centre of Joss Morecombe's kingdom, his domain, where for the past five years he had been plotting, scheming, and controlling everything at Sherwood Strikers. His routine scarcely varied. He was in at 7 o'clock every morning, calm, unruffled, but tackling everything with an energy that three people couldn't have matched. And always doing five things at once.

Joss was at his desk a full hour before anyone else on the management team and four hours before any of the players turned up for training at the practice ground. 'But I know exactly where every one of them is,' he would boast, and who was to say it wasn't true? Joss kept an obsessive eye on his players; he protected them, helped them, guided them. They were his life. And he had fun doing it.

Today he was sorting out a loan spell in the First Division for three of the reserve players, organising a retirement party for Dottie Blackett, the club's catering manager for the past 30 years and one of Joss's favourites, approving training schedules, dealing with a new sponsorship contract, finalising details of tomorrow's flight to Turkey and giving an interview to Katie Moncrieff of the *Mirror*.

Control was Joss's big word. 'Unless you have control, you can't have targets, dreams, visions, in football,' he told Katie as he offered her another slice of toast and marmalade. 'I'm not a control freak, but I've been in positions where I've had no control and that means you've got no time – for anything. You're always chasing around trying to catch up.'

'Except for winning the Cup, your performance was disappointing last season,' said Katie. 'Are you more optimistic this year?'

'We were doing fine until we were hit by

injuries and discipline problems last year,' said Joss. 'This year we've got a stronger squad. The younger players have got some experience under their belts. Take Thomas Headley and Jason Le Braz – this time last year they were pretty green. Now they're top professionals and World Cup heroes. Makes a difference, does that.'

'Aren't you already missing Dave Franchi at the back?'

'Of course we are. I didn't want Dave to go. But he's got his own career to think about and if he's daft enough to want to be a manager, then good luck to him. Between you and me I think he'll be a good one. It's no secret I'm still looking to buy a class defender, but now young Jason Le Braz is playing well I don't think we're under any big pressure.'

'What about the UEFA Cup – have you got a plan for that?'

'Well you know Galatasaray; they'll be tough in Turkey. I've put a lot of faith in the fitness of our squad. Look at Jamie MacLachlan and Brad Trainor – you'll not find two fitter players anywhere in Europe. Fitness matters and we've got Dr Martin on side for us with some of the latest and most effective training ideas. You'll not catch Strikers doing just five a sides and a bit of jogging these days. It's much more scientific than that. We've also got this guy coming over from the States to teach us the latest ideas.'

'Does that mean you'll be making changes to the training staff?'

'Maybe. We've got to move with the times. But you'll have to wait and see on that one.'

'And what about motivation?'

'Motivation's a strange business. It's not an exact science. Footballers are all different people – some are self-motivators like Jamie MacLachlan. Others need coaxing or a stick up the bum. Some need a cause – like patriotism or religion – and the manager can help to create those causes. But the main cause is pride in Sherwood – the town, the people, the team. One thing we've got to sort out is discipline. I want the cleanest team in the country. I want the best behaved players. We had a bit of trouble in that area last season and I hope it's over. At the moment the discipline and team spirit is bloody good. I want us to continue to play the right way.'

Katie looked at him with a smile. 'Who's that message meant for?' she said.

Joss rocked back in his chair with a roar of laughter. 'Trust a canny Scottish lass. Do me a favour and write it anyway.'

Katie Moncrieff was a long-term Strikers fan. She'd become a close friend of Thomas, Jason and Rory and her cool head and her knowledge of the wider football scene had more than once helped the three young players and even the club itself. But Katie kept her support for the Reds a secret. To her readers she had to appear impartial and to be impartial. She filed her article on Joss Morecombe and it appeared on the morning of the Galatasaray game. Two days later, sitting in the press room at the ground after the game in the heat and noise of the Istanbul arena, she wrote a very different report. This is how it appeared in the *Mirror* the next morning:

RED TURKEYS
In a torrid Galatasaray Stadium, the FA Cup holders were outrun, out-staged, and outplayed, by a Turkish side that just knew too much for them. What has happened to Strikers? Why can't they get it together any more?

Yes, it was a rough, tough game. And Strikers were also out-punched, out-shoved and out-kicked in a match where the usual strict rules of refereeing were definitely relaxed. Maybe the ref was intimidated by a hostile crowd. But if he lost

29

his nerve, Strikers lost their heads. Headless turkeys, they were.

Oldie's red card was inevitable, though he was no worse than Kemabal, who downed Headley just outside the box with the most blatant assault from behind without getting even a warning. Headley's ankle injury eventually caused him to leave the field to be replaced by Strikers' new signing, Pahler. Joss Morecombe says Petr Pahler is a player of art and skill – well, he showed neither tonight. But he was not alone in this. I watched as Cecuk and Mirpat on the right and Camlik down the centre all cut through the Strikers' back four like the US Cavalry. If it hadn't been for a brilliant performance in goal by England's Sean Pincher, the Reds would have been four or five down by half time. Even Pincher couldn't keep out Camlik's rocketing header just after the re-start as Cecuk danced past El Harra on the wing. But it wasn't just the defence which was to blame. Where were the Strikers' forwards? Backing into the midfield. Where was the midfield? Pushing back in on the defenders. There was none of the free-running, attacking Sherwood of past seasons. Halfway through the second half Le Braz gave' away a penalty with a late tackle just inside the area and Camlik made no mistake.

The final score of 2-0 was kind to Strikers. It could have been six or seven. Now they have a mountain to climb with the return leg in two weeks' time, but on this form, the UEFA Cup is going to stay safely on the other side of the Channel, if not the other side of Europe.

'We weren't at our best tonight,' said manager Joss Morecombe in the understatement of the year.

'I've been around too long to be fazed by one defeat,' he added. 'We've got some new players to bed in and some work to do but we'll be ready for the home leg.'

After tonight's trouncing, following on from three poor league performances, other people will be asking questions of Morecombe, and wanting straight answers. And action.

Reading that, Thomas Headley felt almost glad he'd picked up his injury in the first half. It was a sprain and the swelling had gone down overnight but there was still a touch of pain. The physios gave him a reassuring report, but he was taken off all but light training for a week and had to undergo regular massage and stretching sessions in the physio unit and some ultra-sound treatment.

Thomas was coming out of the physio room one morning after one of his sessions on the couch when he bumped into Joss Morecombe and Doc Martin. With them was a tall, lanky figure in a white linen suit. The man looked familiar and as he spoke Thomas immediately recognised him. It was PeeWee Wannamaker, the American football coach who had come to their hotel in New Orleans.

'Hi! It's Thomas, isn't it?' PeeWee had a show-man's gift for remembering names. He shook Thomas's hand vigorously. 'They tell me you've picked up some wounds on the battle field. Ankle, eh? I know a great way to help heal an ankle. When you get home, lie down, arms folded across your chest. Let yourself relax, but absolutely relax, all the way down. When you're ready, speak to your cells. These little fellows down there have had a rough time. They've been under pressure. They need to renew themselves. Give them the encouragement they need. Tell them how great they are. It works for you, it works for them. Tell them heal, tell them get whole, tell them you'll reward them with oxygen. You'll be amazed how fast they'll recover. So much is in the mind. Will you do that, Thomas?'

'Erm?' Thomas wasn't sure what to say. This

strange American was telling him to have a long conversation with his foot. Was he having him on? The little Doc was nodding seriously; the boss looked poker-faced as usual.

'I'll check you out tomorrow, Thomas,' said PeeWee Wannamaker. 'Okay?'

He turned to the Doc and Joss. 'We'll let Thomas here show all the other guys what can be done.' And they went on their way.

If that encounter puzzled Thomas, what happened the following day left the entire squad in a state of shock. After the morning practice session, Joss called a team meeting back at Trent Park. Lined up with him were Len Dallal, his deputy coach; Warren Fitzroy, Len's assistant; skipper Jamie MacLachlan; Doc Martin, and none other than PeeWee Wannamaker. Len and Big Mac looked grim. PeeWee gave everyone a sunny smile.

'I just want to let you all know what's happening,' said the boss. 'We're a big organisation, and we need to advance on a lot of different fronts at the same time. Now, the youth side and the school of excellence is our future. We're investing a huge amount of money in it because that's where the core of future teams is going to come from.'

Thomas wondered what was coming next. Why had Joss called together the first team squad to talk about the youth team? It wasn't his style. And what was PeeWee doing there? And then he heard it.

'Len here is going to take charge of the Young Strikers' Academy as the school of excellence will now be called. It's a big job and it needs a big man. Jamie is going to work alongside him and I'll expect every member of the first team squad to put in some time with the youngsters.'

There were a few gasps.

'I'm not saying it's a full-time job for you players,' continued Joss, 'just a couple of hours a week. But if we don't devote some top talent to the Academy, it won't work. And while Len's getting the Academy off the ground, Warren here will step up as acting assistant coach to the first team. Working closely with him will be Doc Martin, whom of course you all know, and Mr Wannamaker here, our special consultant, who will be with us for ten weeks until the end of the year.'

Call me PeeWee,' said the American with a quiet smile.

'Doc Martin and, er, PeeWee will be bringing in

some new methods to assist with training and, especially, motivation. I don't need to go over our last few performances to tell you that motivation needs to be high on the priority list. I expect all of you to give them your full support. Okay, that's it. Any questions?'

He asked in a way that suggested he didn't want to hear any but with Dean Oldie in the audience that was wishful thinking.

'Who's in charge of the team then, Boss?' asked Deano. 'Is it him, or him, or him?' He pointed to Fitzroy, the Doc, and PeeWee.

'I'm in charge of the team,' said Morecombe stonily. 'I'm the manager.'

'But who's taking over Len's job?'

'No one. Any more questions?'

There were none.

But afterwards, there was uproar amongst the players. Jamie MacLachlan, loyal to the core, refused to make any comment on the boss's new appointments.

'Aye ken nae reason why we shouldna gie this PeeWee fella a wee chance,' he said.

'You've changed your tune,' said Psycho. 'And I'll tell you one thing, the little old Doc's in the driving seat. Old Doolally kept him in his place, but Fitzy won't manage it. It's gonna be coconut milk and grits and beans three times a day from now on, lads.'

'And mantras,' said Little Mac. 'Don't forget the mantras.'

'Mantras!' Deano almost spat with disgust. 'I'll get the lads on the Mound to chant a few mantras for him. I can just hear them going, "Ommmm Pasta Fatso Ommmmm".'

'Remember, I no fatso, Psycho,' said Cosimo holding his stomach with pleasure.

'Yeah, it's true – you have lost a bit of weight. I'll take you out for a big plate of pasta tonight.'

'I wonder what PeeWee Wannamaker is costing them,' said Rory. 'He got 10 million bucks from the New Orleans Bays with huge win bonuses on top. I bet he didn't come over here for a free trip to Stratford-upon-Avon.'

'I guess he'll be on a big win bonus,' said Jason.

'Well,' said Perky Trainor, 'maybe it'll work. We're supposed to be one of the richest football clubs in the world so why shouldn't we spend a few bucks? I agree with the skipper: if PeeWee's methods make us winners, I'm not going to complain.'

'If you ask me, ze manageur is going up ze misty mountain waiting for ze wizard with the white beard,' said Paul Claudel, mysteriously.

'If you mean he's lost it, mate, I agree.' It was Drew Stilton. 'Morecombe's been here too long. If he thinks he can treat players like he's treating me he'll soon discover I can do what Dave and Paul did. Leave.'

Yes, Cheesy. Do it, whispered Thomas to himself.

It didn't take long for PeeWee to go 'hands-on'. His first 'Group Talk-In and Thinking Session' wasn't the happiest of introductions.

'I sense a little nervousness and fear here,' said PeeWee who was wearing a brilliant blue track-suit and a red baseball cap. He addressed twenty-six tough and cynical footballers sitting round him with his usual confident smile. 'Bad energy – that's what I want to get rid of. I want you to depend on each other and trust me. Let's convert to something positive. Clanship – good. Suspicion – bad.' He directed each of the players into groups relating to their positional play on the pitch. Thomas stood between Big Mac and Paul Claudel. 'Now I want you each to take each other's hand. Just hold them.'

Twenty-six professional footballers stared back at him, some of them unwilling to believe what they had heard.

'Go on, guys,' he said. 'What's the big deal? Hold hands. I know you're English. Well some of you, at least. But put aside those inhibitions.'

Thomas felt Paul grab his left hand and Jamie his right. A few of the players laughed and coughed uncomfortably.

'Now,' said PeeWee. 'Starting from Thomas here, look at the person on your left – straight into their eyes now.'

Thomas gazed at Paul, who winked at him. 'Keep looking,' said PeeWee. 'Don't watch me. You are friends, you are comrades, you are winners. Say it, "friend, comrade, winner".'

'Friend, comrade, winner,' they muttered in low, embarrassed voices. 'Liberté, Egalité, Fraternité,' said Claudel. 'Vive La France,' and he gave Thomas a huge kiss on the cheek which reduced the whole room to laughter.

When it died away PeeWee smiled at them. 'Well, we've got a lot to achieve, but I believe we can do it. Same time tomorrow, guys. But before you go, you may like to know that I gave Thomas here a little healing mantra for his ankle yesterday. And how's it doing, Thomas?' The bright smile commanded a reply.

Thomas's ankle was indeed almost better, but that was because of the physio sessions. He had totally forgotten PeeWee's advice. He shrugged.

'Fine. The ankle's fine.' He half expected PeeWee to exclaim, Hallelujah, brothers!

4

TURKISH DELIGHT

A draw in the league – this time 2–2 away to Barbican – gave few clues to a settled Sherwood team. Joss experimented with Drew Stilton and Claudel up front and rested Ashleigh who had appeared a little match-weary since the World Cup. Drew scored one of the goals and played well but Claudel and Pahler again had ordinary games. Franco Jordan came on as a sub for Paul Claudel ten minutes from time and got the equalizer – and at least Thomas had the satisfaction of making the pass which put him through on goal, although he hadn't enjoyed the game much otherwise. He still had the feeling that he wasn't getting into the game, even though he felt confident on the ball and was moving well on his ankle. He was substituted 20 minutes from the end of the game.

All was not well at Strikers, he knew that instinctively, yet he found it hard to put his finger on the reasons. However, nothing that happened on or off the pitch prepared Thomas for what he read in the *Post on Sunday* the next day. The headline ran:

A DOG'S LIFE!
That's what Headley leads me at Strikers

Drew Stilton, Sherwood Strikers' controversial international front runner, has come out with an astonishing attack on team-mate Thomas Headley, the star of England's World Cup triumph.

'Headley only plays for himself,' says Stilton. 'He uses me like a brick wall to fire his passes at and then runs on to them and steals all the glory.'

Stilton accuses Headley of being selfish and arrogant. 'None of the players at Sherwood really rate him,' he says. 'Headley treats us all like dogs. We're only here to make him famous – or that's what he thinks. Those two goals in the World Cup final were just flashes in the pan. This season you'll see him like he is. Just an average player who doesn't know how to be part of a team. He only plays for his own mug.'

Thomas was incandescent with rage. He read the article over and over again. 'That's the finish. I can't take any more,' he told Elaine. 'Either Drew Stilton goes or I do. I'm going to tell Joss Morecombe that, unless he gets rid of that creep, I'll be the one to ask for a transfer. I'll go to Italy . . . or Spain. I want you to let the foreign clubs know that I'm up for a move. Tell Morecombe I'm going abroad.'

Elaine remained silent. She knew her son – and she knew how much Drew Stilton's words hurt him. Being his mother and his manager at the same time wasn't always an easy combination. Sometimes it brought conflict. She had hoped that the hatred between the two lads would disperse as they got older and played together, but during and since the World Cup, things had got even worse. She could hardly blame Thomas – he had behaved reasonably well under a lot of provocation. And this last public outburst from Drew was as unforgivable as it was untrue. 'You know that Drew's jealous of your success in the World Cup,' she said at last. 'He's always been jealous of you.'

'Does that give him a right to tell lies like this?'

'No. And I suspect it wasn't all his own idea either.'

'What d'you mean?'

'I mean that his clever manager, Arun Canin, has been looking for a chance to get back at you and me ever since that Club Striker business. When that business deal of his collapsed it cost him a lot of money, you know, and he's a mean, mean person. I bet he's behind this. He's always been very close to the *Post*.'

'Makes no difference to me. I'm not playing on the same side as Drew Stilton. And if you won't tell Joss Morecombe that, then I will.'

'I'll speak to him,' said Elaine wearily. She knew that the Strikers manager was growing tired of Drew's antics but he never took kindly to being told how to run his club by the players or their managers. She'd have to tread very carefully.

In the event Elaine needn't have worried. By the time she saw Joss, Drew had already been disciplined by the club for the *Post* article.

'You can tell young Thomas that Stilton's suspended for three games and fined £15,000 in wages for that daft story. And I've told him he'll be out for much longer unless he writes and apologises to Thomas.'

'I'll believe that when I see it,' said Elaine.

'You'll see. Thomas'll get a proper apology – if Stilton wants to play for Sherwood again, that is. And I suspect he does.'

Elaine enjoyed talking to Joss in the privacy of his den. She both liked and admired the Strikers' manager but this wasn't the relaxed, smiling Joss Morecombe that she was used to. Something was troubling him. 'What's up, Joss?' she asked outright. 'It's not just Drew Stilton who's bothering you, is it?'

Joss sat back. 'To be honest I'm beginning to wonder if I'm too old for this game.'

'That's rubbish.'

'Maybe. But, you see, I've worked alongside Len Dallal for 15 years. And now the chairman and the board and everyone else here think they know more about football than me and him and they're telling me Len's methods are out of date. They might be right. But if he's out of date, so am I.'

'Nonsense.'

'Look at it this way then. Old Len's sidelined to the youth team and hardly talking to me, and who can blame him. Now we've got this touchy-feely geezer over from Yankee land who some people say is the greatest and I don't know whether I'm losing my touch but . . .'

· 'Follow your instincts, Joss. Isn't that what you always say?'

'Yes, but I'm used to motivating English footbailers – well, British, any roads. This bunch is different – we've got British and Yanks and Italians and French and Portuguese and you name it. And that's not all . . . we've got family types and ravers; motorbike enthusiasts and wine experts; aspiring actors and poets and DIY types. I've never known a footie team like it. And what's worse, I chose them all. Don't get me wrong – they're all good players. And mostly a great bunch of lads.'

'Sounds fine to me.'

'Fine? Give me a load of thicko lager louts any day. At least I can understand them. Even Drew Stilton makes some sense to me – he's misbehaving like a footballer. But this lot!'

'So what are you going to do?'

'Sit back and give Doc Martin and his wacky mate PeeWee a chance, I suppose. Maybe I've got something to learn from them. We'll see.'

Strikers earned their first league victory of the season on the Saturday before the home leg against Galatasaray. It was an unconvincing 1-0 home win against Southdown United but it was three points and the goal tapped in by Paul Claude1 took a lot of pressure off the French international. No one, not even the greatest of footballers, finds it easy to live up to a £25 million price tag when they're not playing well.

It was Warren Fitzroy not Joss Morecombe, who announced the team for Wednesday's UEFA Cup game:

Sean Pincher

Jason Le Braz   Brad Trainor   Tarquin Kelly   Ben El Harra

Cosimo Lagattello   Petr Pahler   Jamie MacLachlan   Thomas Headley

Ashleigh Coltrane   Paul Claudel

Reserves: Rory Betts (goal), Ezal Delmonty, Sergio Gambolini, Francisco Panto-Gomes, Franco Jordan, Lanny McEwan.

The capacity crowd at Trent Park were strangely muted for a European game. The sports writers in the morning's papers were not giving Strikers much hope of pulling off a victory and the crowd probably secretly agreed with the press's verdict. The Turkish side were renowned for their tough, uncompromising defence and they were expected to sit on their two-goal advantage. With

Claudel and Coltrane up front, Thomas was looking forward to playing a more attacking role out on the wing. The danger lay in the breakaways and, with Dean Oldie suspended, the back four suddenly looked a lot more fragile.

The atmosphere in the Strikers dressing room was tense but positive.

'Ah wan ya a' tae forget aboot yon horlicks in Turkey and gie a paformance to poot pride in ya hearts,' said Big Mac, before the team funnelled out of the dressing room into the tunnel. 'And Ah wan ya tae play like men not Noo Age wee fairies.' A couple of players laughed. Thomas guessed that 'Noo Age wee fairies' was a jibe at the Doc and PeeWee and the rest of the specialist training team which seemed to grow in numbers every day. 'The white coat barmy army' Psycho called them when he wasn't calling them something a great deal ruder. It was the first time that the skipper had openly criticised the new training regime. That – and Joss Morecombe's unprecedented absence from the dressing room before the kick-off – had most of the team thinking hard. There was a sense of realism and determination about the Strikers side that ran out to encounter Galatasaray.

Things couldn't have started worse. After ten

minutes' play, which was more like the clash of 22 gladiators than a game of football, Ashleigh Coltrane chased a long ball down the right and was met by a fierce sliding tackle by the Turk's big central defender, Kemabal. Ashleigh's leg seemed to buckle under him and he gave a piercing cry of pain. The Galatasaray goalkeeper, realising that Ashleigh was in trouble, booted the ball hard into touch and all the players rushed over to the big No 9 who was lying absolutely still, groaning in agony.

'I've broken it,' he said simply.

The stretcher and Strikers' medical adviser came on and, after a short inspection of the leg, Ashleigh was carried off, covered from head to foot with a large red and white blanket.

The players were shocked by the sudden and terrible injury to their key striker. The incident was all the worse because it had seemed relatively innocuous. Little Mac came on as a straight sub for Ashleigh and the game continued in a hushed atmosphere.

Steadily the work rate rose and Strikers produced more and more attacking football but, time and again, their careful build-ups were snuffed out by the well-disciplined Turkish defence. It was Galatasaray who came closest to scoring in the first 40 minutes when Mirpat was put through by Camlik, managed to turn Perky Trainor and got a shot on goal which Pincher deftly turned round the post.

But just before half time Thomas won the ball in his own half and sprayed a pass right across the pitch to Cosimo who was lurking wide on the right. The Sicilian rode one tackle and centred hard. Little Mac met the cross behind his marker and headed down and on target. The Turkish keeper got down well and parried the shot but, before he could gather it in, Claudel swooped and chipped the ball over him into the back of the net. Suddenly it looked at if there was a way back after all.

At half time there was still no sign of Joss Morecombe in the Strikers dressing room. Warren Fitzroy mumbled a few tongue-tied words and tried to sound up-beat and the Doc stood by him smiling as if he was watching a comedy show that no one else could see. Warren did make one change to the Sherwood line-up, bringing on Sergio Gambolini for Petr Pahler. Sergio would play ahead of Cosimo, giving Jason more opportunities to go on runs down the right wing.

That was the theory. In practice the second half

was more of the same. Careful building and possession football by Strikers; tough, resolute defending by Galatasaray. Kemabal, their big centre back, was in the heart of it all. Thomas had good cause to remember his crude tackle from behind in the first leg and both Claudel and Little Mac discovered that the big defender didn't take hostages. Half way through the second half he was given a yellow card for a professional foul, tugging Claudel's shirt when he was clean through. For some officials it would have been a sending-off offence.

The crowd, which had started to get behind the Reds after the re-start, was becoming more and more frustrated. Warren Fitzroy threw on Franco Jordan for Lagattello with ten minutes to go in a final desperate bid to get the second goal. Then with five minutes left Ben El Harra hobbled off with a knee injury and Panto-Gomes replaced him. Somehow the midfield held its shape; there was no panic in spite of the fans' chant:

> 'Hello, hello, where are the Reds?
> They're tired and they want to go to bed.'

Thomas received a pass out on the wing from Trainor, who had had a towering game in defence. He took the ball past two tackles and then cut back onto his right foot. As Kemabal slid in with all studs showing, Thomas deftly side-stepped and found Claudel with a pass which split two defenders. The big Frenchman shrugged off a tackle and fired past the defiant Turkish keeper for his second of the night.

The crowd leapt to its feet; the biggest roar so far echoed round the ground. But a minute later there was an even louder one. Thomas again started the movement and then cut the ball back to Big Mac who dummied to go on the outside and switched down the middle. His pass was beautifully paced for Little Mac to run onto and the forward lifted a perfect chip over the advancing keeper. Kemabal chased back desperately but his overhead kick on the goal line only succeeded in hoofing the ball into the roof of the net. Three–nil.

Strikers survived a nasty scare at the other end when Camlik broke on goal and hit the crossbar. Then at last the final whistle sounded. They had won the tie 3–2 on aggregate – against all the odds.

As they walked off, exchanging shirts with the Galatasaray players, Thomas noticed the face of Len Dallal in the crowd, sitting slightly aside

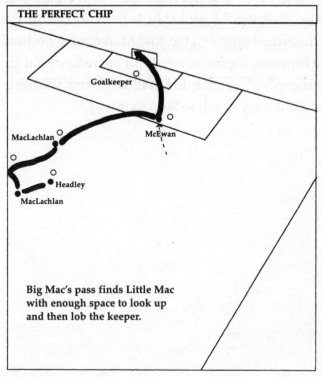

THE PERFECT CHIP

Goalkeeper

MacLachlan

McEwan

Headley

MacLachlan

**Big Mac's pass finds Little Mac
with enough space to look up
and then lob the keeper.**

● Sherwood Strikers
○ Galatasaray

from the subs bench. He was wrapped in his red scarf and clapping the players' performance more enthusiastically than anyone in the ground. No doubt about where old Doolally's loyalties lie, thought Thomas. But what would this result mean for him? The Doc and PeeWee were bound to claim it as a victory for their weird methods. And that would probably leave Len out in the wilderness forever. Had Joss Morecombe decided to bow out, too? And what did the future hold for Strikers? More holding hands? More Clanship stuff? It very much looked that way.

5

LEARNING CURVE

'This is it?' asked Thomas Headley, in a disbelieving voice.

'Yeah,' said Warren Fitzroy.

'The apology? The great apology?'

Warren looked slightly embarrassed. He gazed at the ceiling for a moment, then sniffed. 'It's very difficult, you know. Drew's got his pride; he's already been disciplined by the club. What more do you want? Blood?'

Thomas looked at him coldly. 'No. Just an honest apology. Listen to this:

"I'm sorry if Thomas Headley has taken offence at my words in the Post on Sunday *when my intention was never to embarrass or offend but only to encourage him to play a more co-operative game in future in the interest of the club."* It's pathetic.'

'Well he says "I'm sorry" – that's . . .'

'Not an apology at all and you know it. And I don't believe he even wrote this rubbish. "Intention", "embarrass", "co-operative" – he doesn't even know what those words mean.'

Thomas had been summoned to Trent Park by Warren Fitzroy and Pete Frame, the club's smooth-talking press and PR man. Pete and Warren sat on one side of the desk, Thomas and Elaine on the other. So far Elaine hadn't said a word. Pete Frame was all for a compromise. He was hoping to arrange a photocall with Drew and Thomas shaking hands but Thomas was in no mood for compromises.

'The thing is, Thomas,' said Frame, leaning back in his chair, 'if you go off in a huff, it puts you in a bad light, if you see what I mean?'

'Listen,' said Thomas, fighting down his rage. 'You're the press officer and you know the truth. Why don't you just tell it like it is: Stilton won't apologise. And until he does I'm not playing with him, training with him or going within a hundred miles of him. Is that plain?'

Elaine put a hand gently on his shoulder. She opened her briefcase and brought out a neatly-typed sheet. 'I've had this prepared by our lawyers,' she said. 'If Stilton signs it we'll let the matter drop. Otherwise we're going to take it to the Football Players Association. We'll see if we can get some straight talking from them.'

'Give us a few minutes,' said Warren Fitzroy. He and Pete Frame went out.

'Do you think we've gone too far?' asked Thomas quietly when they were alone.

'I doubt it. My guess is that they've got Stilton and Arun Canin in the next room and they're sweating it out. But where's Joss? He should be handling this. Not Warren and smoothy Pete.'

Minutes later the two officials returned. Pete Frame was smiling as usual, and Warren looked more worried than ever.

'Will this do?' asked Warren, holding out another sheet of paper. Elaine and Thomas read it together.

'I am sorry if my words caused any offence to Thomas Headley, and I withdraw any suggestion that he is not a complete team player.'

'No, it won't do,' said Elaine crisply. Thomas looked at her uncertainly. Gritting their teeth, the two left the room again. A longer wait this time but eventually they returned. Elaine took the sheet they held out. It was the one she had brought with her. She read aloud:

'I completely withdraw the untrue and offensive statements made by me about my team-mate Thomas Headley in the Post *on Sunday. I accept that they do not contain a shred of truth and I apologise unreservedly to him and to Strikers FC, and deeply regret the distress my comments may have created.'*

It was signed with a slashing, viciously scrawled *Drew Stilton.*

'I couldn't have put it better myself,' said Elaine with a faint smile as she looked again at her own words on the paper in front of her.

'Then we'll draw a line under the whole incident,' said Pete Frame. 'No press statement, no pictures.'

'Not quite,' said Elaine. 'We'd like a copy of this released to the press.'

'But they'll publish it . . .' began Pete Frame. His smile even switched off for a second.

'Very well,' said Warren. 'We agree.'

'Then that's all settled,' said Elaine. 'But I just want to say one thing. We shouldn't have had to battle like this to get proper treatment. After all, an apology was what Joss Morecombe promised me and I expect him to be a man of his word. And, in my opinion he should have been here sorting this one out.'

Warren and Pete looked nervously at each other. 'The manager's too busy right now,' said Warren uncertainly. 'He's got a lot on at the moment.'

Elaine shook her head, got up, shook hands with the two men and walked out of the office. Thomas followed closely behind her.

That afternoon Thomas had a date he didn't dare miss. Strikers Juniors were playing Highfield Rovers Juniors. And in the Highfield side his little brother Richie would be wearing the number 10 shirt.

Elaine, Katie Moncrieff, Jason and Rory had all received their orders to be there, too. Richie was determined that his moment of glory would be witnessed by his mum, his brother and his brother's best friends at Strikers. 'Unbeaten all season,' said Richie virtually every time he saw Thomas. 'We'll give Strikers a good hiding today,' he told Katie. 'I hope you're going to write about it.'

'Of course I am,' said Katie. 'Remind me,

what's the name of your top scorer?' She winked at Thomas.

'It's me, of course. Richie Headley,' said Richie. 'Eleven goals in all competitions so far this season.'

'Don't encourage him,' said Thomas. 'His head's too big for his baseball cap already. And give him half a chance and he'll tell you every detail of all 11 goals.'

Richie ran off to join his team-mates and his fans took their place in the little temporary stand. The Strikers Academy ground was something of a building site these days with new training facilities going up and a new mini stand. Only a handful of people had come along to watch the midweek game. Across the pitch Thomas noticed Len Dallal in his red tracksuit handing out last-minute advice to the young Strikers players. The Highfield team was limbering up in front of the goal to their right.

The ref's whistle finally brought the sides together and a few moments later the match began.

'Don't they look small,' said Rory.

A heavy hand fell on his shoulder from behind. 'Ye were jist a wee yin once yersel.' Big Mac clambered over the seat-back and sat down beside them.

Thomas found himself gripped by the game from the start. It took him back to his own days as a youth player for Newlynn City. These lads were good – better, if anything, than the standard in his day. What really impressed him was their organisation and work rate.

He knew Richie was a good young player but even he hadn't realised he was this good. Thomas watched him running into space, anticipating moves, changing the direction of play. He was already a very sophisticated footballer – and yet he was only 13. But Richie wasn't alone – there were plenty of remarkable talents on display. Bran Thompson, for instance, the captain of the young Strikers, was a big, powerful player with plenty of class. He gave Strikers the lead with a cracking volley after a well-worked build-up. The divided loyalty of the supporters sitting with Thomas soon became clear. They cheered every time Richie touched the ball. But they also stood up and chanted when Strikers scored.

And it was soon apparent that the red shirts were out-playing the black-and-whites. The midfield battle was dominated by the young Strikers and Richie, up front, was getting very little service. Katie kept a note for Richie of shots on goal, completed passes and fouls. By the end of the first half, with the score still 1–0, it looked like this:

	Shots on target	Completed passes	Fouls
Strikers	12	40	5
Rovers	5	29	6

The second half opened with a bang. Thomas jumped out of his seat as he watched Richie take a long ball on his chest, turn, and volley with his left foot. The ball rocketed into the net with exquisite timing. It was a great opportunist goal against the run of play.

'What control! He's better than you,' said Rory to Thomas.

'Wow! That was some goal,' said Katie after they'd all sat back in their seats.

'He can play all right,' said Thomas, trying to sound cool. 'Maybe he's a bit flash at times though.'

Katie elbowed him in the ribs. 'What you mean is, he should play like you! Well, the best thing about Richie's game is that he's doing his own thing. I think he's a natural goal scorer. And goal scorers have to be a bit greedy.'

Big Mac joined Len on the touch line. They had worked hard together on the organisation of their young team and and they watched the play like a pair of hawks. In spite of Richie's equalizer, the Reds were still controlling the game and the patient build-up and possession football soon put them ahead again. The pressure built up and from a corner kick, Bran Thompson broke free and nodded the ball past the keeper.

With five minutes to go Strikers scored a third goal from a free kick on the edge of the area. 3–1 was a fair reflection of the play. Thomas was impressed with the skills and understanding that old Doolally had built up amongst his young charges in such a short time. He was also a bit relieved that Strikers had won. Richie was a little subdued after the game, which was not a bad thing after all the crowing of recent weeks. But he soon bucked up when Katie congratulated him on his goal.

'Yeah, a bit special, wasn't it?' he said.

Waiting for Richie to change, Thomas took the chance to have a word with Len Dallal. Old Doolally greeted him like an old friend. They hadn't seen much of each other since the reorganisation although, like the other first team players, Thomas had put in a few sessions with the Juniors on the training pitch.

'Great little team you've got here. They've got real class,' said Thomas.

'They're learning,' Len agreed and then after a pause, 'learning to be football players, not Buddhist monks.'

'Have you seen anything of the boss?' asked Thomas as casually as he could.

'Not a sign since he packed me off here to Siberia to work with the babes. That's the way I like it. Here I do it my own way and by the time I'm finished, it's going to be the top youth side in the country.'

'No one's seen much of Joss. He's become a bit of a hermit.'

'Morecombe is a good man,' said Len, after a pause. 'And I rate him the best manager in the country – I've never made any secret of that. But even a great manager can go through a sticky time. He's afraid of being left behind in the modern world, afraid of losing the plot. Me, I don't care. I know what I'm good at, and you can see the results out here. But I don't have his responsibilities. The Gaffer's a survivor, though. He'll be back. And then – look out. The man's a phenomenon. Sooner or later we'll all see some fireworks from him. I just hope it's before that Yank wrecks all the hard work we've put in together to build up a winning football team.'

He gave Thomas a slap on the back and walked off to talk to his young players about the game.

6
CRISIS

	P	W	L	D	F	A	Pts
West Thames Wanderers	8	5	0	3	15	5	18
Highfield Rovers	8	5	1	2	15	7	17
Newlynn City	7	5	1	1	18	9	16
Barbican	7	4	0	3	14	6	15
Derwent Athletic	7	4	0	3	15	10	15
St James	7	4	1	2	16	8	14
Danebridge Forest	8	3	1	4	13	9	13
Mersey United	8	4	4	0	14	15	12
Branston Town	8	2	1	5	11	14	11
Border Town	8	2	2	4	12	13	10
Kingstown Academy	7	3	3	1	13	15	10
White Hart United	7	2	2	3	10	10	9
Southdown United	8	1	1	6	10	11	9
Wierdale Harriers	8	2	3	3	13	16	9
Fenland Rangers	7	2	4	1	7	12	7
Mersey City	7	1	3	3	9	16	6
Sherwood Strikers	**7**	**1**	**4**	**2**	**7**	**12**	**5**
Wednesfield Royals	8	1	5	2	8	15	5
Alexandra Park	8	1	6	1	6	12	4
Wyvern Vale	8	0	5	3	4	15	3

Six weeks into the new season and Strikers' Premier League form had hit rock bottom. There was already talk of relegation, which would have been utterly unthinkable at the start of the season. But the results in the league spoke for themselves.

St James 3 – Sherwood Strikers 1
West Thames Wanderers 1 – Sherwood Strikers 0
Sherwood Strikers 1 – Weirdale Harriers 1
Barbican 2 – Sherwood Strikers 2
Sherwood Strikers 1 – Southdown United 0
Wednesfield Royals 2 – Sherwood Strikers 1
Newlynn City 3 – Sherwood Strikers 1

With big games ahead against Fenland Rangers and Highfield Rovers at home and Danebridge Forest away, there was a fair chance that the slump would continue. Only two points separated them from the bottom club, newly promoted Wyvern.

Thomas's own feelings about the morale at the club had plummeted further after the game against his old team' Newlynn City. Newlynn had also just been promoted to the Premier League as Division One champions. It wasn't so much losing to them that bothered Thomas but the way they had lost. Katie Moncrieff had got it just about right in the *Mirror* when she wrote:

Strikers were desperate. Things are so bad the Samaritans seem to have stopped taking their phone calls. How can a team with such great international stars as Claudel, MacLachlan, Headley, Lagattello, Le Braz play like they've just met on the bus? The passing was atrocious, the marking a joke, the movement sideways and, worst of all, no one seemed to care.

Most of the team were well aware of the reason for Strikers' decline, of course, but no one seemed to know what to do about it. If morale on match days was bad, it was even worse at practice sessions. Everyone was arguing about everything: what to do, how long to practise set-pieces, what drinks they had. It got so bad that a niggly little row between Tarquin Kelly and Paul Claudel turned into a full-scale brawl and the Frenchman stormed out with a bloody nose. Worse still, a freelance photographer got a picture of him leaving.

Joss Morecombe remained cut off from his team and from virtually everyone in the club. He would arrive at the ground punctual as ever at 7 o'clock and shut himself away in his den. He hardly spoke to a soul all day except to bark a few orders over the phone. He was spotted from time to time as he arrived at and left Trent Park but he talked to none of the players – not even Big Mac. Then, inevitably, came the rumours that the club's board were threatening him with dismissal.

'The gaffer's got three matches to turn it round or it's the sack,' said Psycho.

'Who told you that?' asked Ben El Harra.

'Maeve did. And she's always right.' Maeve Anderson was Ronnie the head groundsman's wife. She was in charge of catering, cleaning and virtually everything at the club, and knew more about what was going on than the boss himself. If she said Joss's job was on the line, it probably was.

When they were together in the evening Thomas, Jason and Rory talked about little else but the crisis at Strikers and how to get rid of PeeWee and the white coats. Jason and Rory had come round to agreeing with Thomas and most of the rest of the team that PeeWee's methods were doing a lot more damage than good – but it was Joss's absence which worried all of them most of all.

'Some of PeeWee's ideas might work in the right place,' said Jason. 'But he doesn't know a thing about football – or soccer, as he calls it.'

'It's like everyone's in the wrong job,' said Rory. 'We've got Doc Martin picking the team when he should be doing fitness and diet; Warren Fitzroy, who's great on the practice field but can't get two words in the right order, looking after tactics and motivation; and Old Doolally, the best coach in the country, running the junior team. Joss Morecombe, the heart and soul of the club, has become a recluse. The whole thing's topsy turvy.'

'And behind the scenes PeeWee's running everything. He's the only one Doc listens to,' said Jason.

'At least we know where we are with PeeWee,' said Rory. 'He's a nutter. Simple as that. Did you see him on TV last night?'

'Yeah. I liked the bit about all the team eating those special short bananas flown in from Sri Lanka,' said Thomas. PeeWee Wannamaker had appeared on a late night chat show to air his famous training theories. He'd talked and talked about mantras and Clanship and hugging and food supplements like 'creatine' and faith healers and aromatherapy and the foreign legion and the

Alamo. But he never once talked about football.

'Did you see what the *Post* is calling us today?' said Jason. 'Sherwood Strokers.'

'They say we'd make a superb Morris dancing team,' said Thomas. 'And did you hear the latest song on the terraces? It starts like this:

"Take my hand, take my whole life too,
We'll see you next, down in Division Two."'

'Yes, I've heard it. It gets a bit rude after that,' said Jason with a grin.

'It's time we had a plan,' said Rory. 'PeeWee's got to go – or we've got to get rid of him before we're relegated or worse. And Joss Morecombe has got to get a grip or he's out. Someone needs to make him see sense.'

'How can we do that if he won't even talk to us?' asked Jason.

'I've got a sort of idea,' said Rory.

Thomas and Jason looked at him cautiously. Rory had good ideas and bad ideas – and they were always a little crazy.

Meanwhile the situation at Strikers was descending into high farce. PeeWee still had a few loyal supporters amongst the players – Perky Trainor and Tarquin Kelly were perhaps the most enthusiastic and they continued to support PeeWee's weird training methods. Drew Stilton pretended to be on their side too, but Drew would probably have sided with the Prince of Darkness rather than agree with Thomas Headley. Doc Martin was, of course, still 100% behind Peewee and his troop of specialist dietitians, therapists and masseurs grew every day.

'It's like MI5,' said Psycho. 'I reckon all these geezers in white coats are really the Doc's private spy network. And I can prove it. I told that blond Australian aromatherapist that Big Mac's going to play Robert the Bruce in a new Hollywood film and what happens? Every day this week the Doc's been after him for his autograph for his kids.'

'And who told the story about me being disciplined for modelling naked in *True Grit* magazine?' asked Brad Trainor.

'I said it was in the best possible taste, Perky,' said Psycho.

'But I never did it!'

'It's all in the interests of the club, Perky. We need to know how these lies get spread around.'

'They get spread around because you start them,' complained Brad. 'I keep getting strange phone calls asking me what my modelling rates are.'

'Put them on to me. I'll get you a good deal.' Psycho was never lost for words. But on this occasion most of the players agreed there was a serious purpose behind his practical jokes. He was determined to make the Doc and PeeWee look as ridiculous as possible. His biggest joke was also his best.

On Thursday morning, one of the rare occasions in the week when the team got to kick a ball about on the practice pitch, Warren Fitzroy found his training session interrupted by an invasion of Druids dressed in long white flowing robes who said they'd been sent by PeeWee to introduce the team to the mysteries of early Clanship. They told the team to sit down in a circle, whereupon they brought on some plastic replicas of the stones at Stonehenge and started dancing around them and chanting in a most blood-curdling way. One by one the players and Warren Fitzroy and the Doc were dragged into the dance which got faster and faster until a Druid selected Drew Stilton to be a sacrifice on the high altar. Flashing knives appeared and Drew went very pale and started to struggle.

'It's okay,' said the Doc, trying to be helpful.

'What they are doing is testing your commitment to the team, isn't that right?'

One of the Druids grunted and floored the Doc with a rugby tackle. 'We kill the little fat one, too,' he said. The Doc, looking increasing terrified, was bound hand and foot. It was at this point that one of the Druids' beard fell off and Big Mac recognised Psycho's dad. Everyone except Warren, Drew Stilton and the Doc fell about in helpless laughter.

Meanwhile, as Psycho amused himself at the expense of the white coats, Rory, Thomas and Jason were working on The Plan. At first sight Rory's idea seemed completely off the wall and Thomas thought if they went ahead with it they'd be lucky to avoid being sacked or even arrested. Katie Moncrieff was taken into their confidence, mainly at Thomas's insistence, because he thought she might have a better and more sensible idea. But, somewhat to his surprise, Katie gave it the thumbs up too. After that there was no going back. It was decided that they would make their move after Saturday's home game against Fenland Rangers, in which both Jason and Thomas were playing.

The atmosphere in the ground before Saturday's game was both hostile and light-hearted. The fans were angry, but they were doing their best to cheer themselves up. They had picked up quickly on the more absurd things that were happening to their club and, although they didn't like the pattern of results, they tackled events in their usual way. The terrace songs were completely up to date. As Strikers ran out to face Fenland Rangers they were met by the latest lyrics.

'Four banana, three banana, two banana, one,
All bananas playing in the bright warm sun,
Big Mac, Little Mac, DD and Jaws
We like bananas, more, more, more.
Karma, karma, karma, karma, karma, come
    on, you Reds
Come on, you Reds, give us an OMMMMM-
    MMMM!

There's a circus in the town
And Doc Martin is the clown
He is small and he is round
So let's kick him out of town.'

The songs ran into each other, but the theme was the same each time. The Fenland players had never heard anything like it before. They were a tough, physical side and they'd come to Trent

Park for the full three points. With two big forwards up front and their long ball method – often missing out the midfield – they posed a strong aerial threat to the Strikers' back four. Ben El Harra was out with 'flu, so Tarquin Kelly joined Brad Trainor, Dean Oldie and Jason Le Braz at the back and it was Tarquin who missed an overhead kick clearance and allowed big Graham Barlow a clear shot on goal. He put it away clinically to Sean's left.

The boos and the jeers stung Strikers into action and they had three or four chances to draw level before half time but the keeper or the bar or the uprights kept them out. When things are going downhill your luck deserts you too.

The Doc stood before them at half time smiling and telling them they were playing well, really well, but they needed to play for each other more. After a performance like that Joss Morecombe would have slammed the dressing room door and their ears would have rung with his torrents of angry abuse. But the Doc smiled his strange smile and Warren Fitzroy stood by, silent and bemused. They didn't seem even to have noticed that Brad Trainor was limping from a late tackle and showed no signs of considering substituting him.

As they walked back onto the pitch for the second half to a chorus of boos and OMMMMs, Jamie MacLachlan gave them all a bit of a gee up. 'Ah want ta see a canny bit more aggression frae the Reds or we'll a' be off ter the broo,' he said tersely. 'We'll no be bottom of the heap while I'm skipper here.'

Thomas found it hard to keep his mind on the game, wondering exactly what Rory and Katie were up to. But, after he was clattered by one of the Fenland defenders he put in a stunning, curving ball from the set-piece and Franco Jordan rose above his two markers and headed home. In the final minutes, with Strikers powering forward for the winner, Little Mac was brought down on the edge of the area. Up stepped Cosimo Lagattello to take the penalty. Pasta was the stand-in penalty taker for Ashleigh. He looked confident enough as he placed the ball on the spot and stepped back but his fierce shot hammered into the crossbar and Fenland scrambled it clear. After that the final whistle was something of a relief for the Strikers players and the fans, most of whom had already streamed out of the stadium in silence or chanting a low OMMMMMM.

The team stalked back to the home dressing

room and, as they gloomily filed in, Thomas's mobile rang. He'd been expecting the call and he picked it up quickly with a glance at Jason.

'Hi, it's Katie. It's started.'

'Where are you?'

'In Joss's office. Rory and I are here with the manager. He's not very happy, but there you go. There are five players outside the door: Brian Robinson, Curtis Cropper, Francisco Panto-Gomes, Haile Reifer and Ashleigh on his crutches. Remember, follow the plan – Jason stays there and tells the lads what's going on. They're all welcome to come and join in if they want. You get over here straightaway. I want you to be here when we ask him the big question.'

Thomas put his mobile down slowly. He looked up at the other players. 'The boss has been hijacked,' he said suddenly. A few of the players thought it was another bad joke, and laughed.

'Good one, DD,' said Psycho. 'Pity they didn't get the Doc and PeeWee, too.'

'We're holding him under house arrest,' said Thomas.

'And that's where he stays until he agrees to some changes,' added Jason.

Something about the seriousness of the two

young players' voices made their colleagues stop and listen.

'I'm off to join the kidnappers,' said Thomas. 'Jace, tell them all about it.' And he hurried out of the dressing room still wearing his match kit.

7
'SOCCER'S HAD IT'

Outside the manager's office, the famous five, Robbo, Curtis, Cisco, Haile and Ashleigh with his leg in plaster and on crutches, were standing guard. They gave Thomas a cheer and a pat or two on the back as he walked past them.

'Don't let him wriggle out of this, whatever you do,' said Ashleigh. 'We're all behind you.'

'He doesn't leave until he gives in,' said Curtis Cropper. 'If it takes all season, we stay here.'

Joss Morecombe stared angrily at Thomas as he entered the den. The little room seemed packed already even though there were only three people in it. Joss Morecombe was quietly munching away at a ham, mustard and cress sandwich. Opposite him sat Katie and Rory. Joss looked calm enough, almost as if he reckoned that being hijacked by his players was an everyday event. Thomas gave him a sheepish grin.

'So are you going to tell me what this little jape is all about, Thomas, lad?' asked Joss. 'Your mates here seem to have lost the power of speech.'

Thomas looked at Rory and then at Katie. Rory nodded a welcome and then turned to the manager. It was time to deliver their ultimatum.

'You know what we want, Boss,' said Rory firmly. 'And before you start accusing the other players, this was our idea, not theirs.'

'Your idea,' insisted Katie. She looked Joss in the eye. 'And I think it's a good one, too.'

'What?' said Joss, through a mouthful of sandwich. 'My players break every disciplinary rule in the book and you call it a good idea? It isn't *Bonnie and Clyde* or *Thelma and Louise*, you know. If you've set this up for your rag to make a big story out of it, I'll make sure you're the one who is driven out of town, lass.'

'I'm not doing this for the story. There won't be a story. I'm doing it because I'm a Strikers fan. That's why I'm here.'

'I've never understood fans,' said Joss. 'First you tell me I'm out of touch. And now you're complaining because I've brought in some new ideas. What's so wrong with giving the new system a fair chance? Results don't come overnight.'

'Because you'll be kicked out if things carry on like this. Don't you understand that?' said Katie.

Joss sighed. 'I've been in football a long time. But this is the first time I've faced up to a players' revolt headed up by a lass to stop me being fired. OK, you've had your little joke. I've heard the message. Now get out of my office.'

Nobody moved.

Joss Morecombe took a deep breath. His face flushed pink and he walked to the door. It was locked. He reached for the telephone. It was dead. He fiddled in his desk for his mobile and when he realised it was missing he slumped back angrily in his seat.

'PeeWee's got to go,' said Thomas suddenly. It was the first time he had spoken.

'What do you know about it, son?' snapped Joss. 'You're still wet behind the ears. You leave the managing to me and try and remember why we hired you. To play football. Recall?'

'Maybe this will help you understand what's going on round here,' said Rory. He produced a small tape recorder, placed it on the manager's desk, and turned it on. For a moment there was no sound except a faint hiss. Then the deep southern drawl of PeeWee Wannamaker broke in.

'Hi, Rory. What can I do for you?'

'I just wanted to say that I think your ideas are fantastic. I just wish everyone in the club would appreciate what you're trying to achieve here.'

'Hey, yeah, I know. Some guys will never have it in them to understand, and until we get rid of them we won't get the results. They'll have to go. Simple as that. We know who they are, right?'

'I know who you're talking about – but what about Joss? He won't stand by while you and Doc sack his players.'

'Hey, Rory, we know Joss is a great guy. But, Rory, tell me, does he have belief?'

'What d'you mean?' said Rory.

'He's a man who's lost his way. Typical old generation soccer man. What Joss doesn't know is that the soccer he was brought up on is dead. It's had its day. This is the age of world sport. Baseball, football, basketball, soccer – they're all the same. Performance sports. We don't want soccer players any more. We want stars, athletes, team men. You understand that, Rory – you're an American.'

'Sure, PeeWee.'

'I rate some of the young guys around here. But there are a lot of old attitudes that have got to go. And Joss Morecombe belongs to the past. Until Strikers takes on board the new ideas and chucks out the old it's going nowhere.'

Rory reached over and clicked the recorder off. 'There's plenty more of the same if you want to hear it,' he said.

Joss looked pensive. Then he spoke. ' I didn't bring him over to tell me how lovely I am,' he said. 'If he thinks I'm old fashioned, fair enough. All I want is what's best for Strikers and they tell me PeeWee did a good job with the New Orleans Bears or Bees or whatever they're called.'

'Bays.'

'And don't you think that bugging him was a bit of a dirty trick?' Joss asked Rory.

'Just returning the favour,' said Rory.

'What do you mean?'

Rory leaned past him and looked down at the skirting board. 'Here you are.'

He held a little grey metal object in his hand. 'Neat one. Voice activated. Hi, PeeWee, how's it going?'

Joss's eyebrows almost disappeared into his luxuriant grey hair. When he spoke, his voice was different. 'So what are the demands?' he asked.

'No demands,' said Rory. 'We just want you to see sense. You don't come along to practice session or the games any more and so you don't see the nonsense going on. The Strikers are becoming a joke.'

'We want you back in charge,' said Thomas.

'And Len Dallal running the practice sessions again,' said Katie.

'And if I don't agree?'

'We stay here till you do,' said Katie. 'Even if it means missing my deadline or the next Strikers game or the whole season. Because we all believe this club will go nowhere unless you take charge again.'

'I'm not God around here,' said Morecombe, 'I'm just the manager. All this new training stuff is official board policy.'

'They'll change it if you face them with the consequences,' said Katie. 'No manager and no team.'

A silence fell over the little room. Joss looked at his captors one by one. Then the key turned in the lock, the door burst open and the rest of the first team poured in. It was like an attempt on the world record for the number of people in a telephone kiosk. For a time there was chaos as everyone spoke at once. Then Joss raised his hands and there was silence.

'I take it you all support this ridiculous prank,'

he said.

There was a roar of approval from the players.

'Hush,' shouted Big Mac. 'Will ya no listen tae the gaffer?'

Joss Morecombe stood up. 'I'll not pretend that I'm a great believer in democracy when it comes to football clubs,' he said, 'but I can't see that I've got much choice on this occasion. I'd have a tough time finding another team before Wednesday night. But first I'd like to hear the skipper's views.'

All eyes turned to Big Mac. 'It's nae a joke, Boss,' he said. 'We a' ken thon new system disnae work. Tha yonkie mon disnae nae a thang aboot fitba' and the wee Doc's as mad as an Hibs supporter.'

Joss smiled for the first time. The warm, infectious smile that had been missing for weeks. 'Okay, it's agreed. But I want terms. You may think I'm not in a position to bargain but many's the time I've thought of walking away from this club in the past few weeks. I don't think I'd be short of offers. And, from what I understand, you don't want that. So if you want me to stay you'd better listen.'

'Agreed,' said Katie quickly before any of the players could butt in.

'Then the first thing you do is give me my mobile so that I can book us all into a decent restaurant. We'll talk about this in the private room of the Shoemaker's Arms. The sooner we all get out of this cupboard the better.'

'You're the Boss,' said Rory, passing over the phone.

8

HAMMER AND SICKLE

On Monday morning, Thomas Headley drove up to Trent Park. He had already bought all the newspapers, half expecting to see headlines such as 'Showdown at Sherwood' and 'Strikers Players Revolt'. But there was nothing apart from the match report on the Fenland game which he didn't much feel like reading. The big sports news story, if you could call it that, was about another financial crisis at Sultan Palace. As he drove in through the players' entrance the security guard stopped him.

'Big emergency board meeting on,' he said. 'All the bigwigs are here. Something's up.' He winked at Thomas as if to tell him that he knew more than he was letting on. Strikers was a close-knit family club and news travelled fast. Maeve Anderson had almost certainly been feeding the grapevine. 'Good luck,' said the guard as Thomas drove on.

Training had been postponed till the afternoon and all the players were asked to report to the ground. Something was up all right. Thomas just hoped that Joss would carry out his promises and, more importantly, that the board would still be prepared to back him.

'Team meetin' in the video room. Ha' past eleven,' said Big Mac who was the first player Thomas saw.

One by one the players wandered in and took their seats. On the dot of 11.30 Joss Morecombe stalked in with the club's chairman Monty Windsor. Joss was looking relaxed but giving nothing away; Monty was looking a little weary – it had been a long and bruising board meeting.

'I have a brief statement from the board which relates to training at the club,' began Monty hesitantly. 'It goes like this. "The board reiterates its policy that training methods and the hiring of personnel and players shall be the sole responsibility of the manager both on a day to day basis and in terms of policy." '

'And what does that gobbledygook mean?' asked Psycho.

'It means that there has been some unfortunate

interference in management by some members of the board and in future that will cease. The manager has our full support and he picks the team and the back-up staff.'

Joss's face creased into a smile. 'It means I'm in charge. Psycho. So watch out.'

There was a loud cheer from the players and Monty raised his hands for silence. 'There's one more thing. Joss Morecornbe's contract has been extended but the board feels that it should reserve the right to look at the team's position in the league at its next meeting and review the situation.' Monty sat down, pulled out a handkerchief and mopped his brow.

Joss got to his feet. There was a gleam in his eye that his players had not seen for a long time. He looked like a man who had just won a big battle.

'You heard the chairman,' he said. 'It's business as usual. If you want another translation I'd say the board are giving me enough rope to hang myself. If we're still in the bottom half of the league by Christmas, I'll be taking a long walk off a short plank. So it's up to you to perform to your ability if you want my ugly mug to remain around here. If you've got any questions, ask them now or step into my office, But not all together this time, please.'

*

Doc Martin and Warren Fitzroy were the sole survivors of the reshuffle which was announced at the end of the morning. The troop of special advisers, counsellors, spiritual guides and nutritionists who had run the show at Strikers over the recent weeks just melted away. The abrupt disappearance of PeeWee Wannamaker hardly created a stir; no one saw him again. One moment he was everywhere and the next he'd vanished without trace.

To nobody's surprise, the Doc was completely unrepentant about the whole business. 'Another month would have brought results,' he complained to Thomas and anyone else prepared to listen.

The Doc was back on his diet and exercise brief, and although a prouder man might have resigned, he carried on with all his usual crazy enthusiasm. He soon threw himself into a new cause: he began writing a book. *The Doc's Football Fitness Manual* became his new obsession and he shrewdly realised that if he lost his job with Strikers it wouldn't be the best-selling success he believed he deserved.

As for the team, fixtures were crowding in on them. A home game on Wednesday against Highfield Rovers was followed by the local derby at Danebridge Forest. Then two more Premier League games in the following week against Branston Town and Derwent Athletic.

But most importantly, Doolally was back. There were only two practice sessions before the Highfield game but they allowed Len Dallal and Joss Morecombe to put their stamp of authority back on the team – and tough sessions they were. Old Doolally had picked up a few new ideas during his spell with the juniors and one of them was what he called 'the hammer and sickle'. It was yet another plan for defeating the wall in a free-kick situation just outside the area. Claudel and Big Mac stood over the ball with four or five players fanned out in a semi-circle to the left of the wall and Jason Le Braz in position on the right – he was the hammer. Big Mac ran over the ball, dummying to pass to the four players of the sickle and then Claudel passed out to Jason who immediately whipped in a cross as the four players of the sickle moved in on goal. It was a fairly complicated manoeuvre but they practised it hard along with a variation which the boss suggested and it served them well in the games ahead.

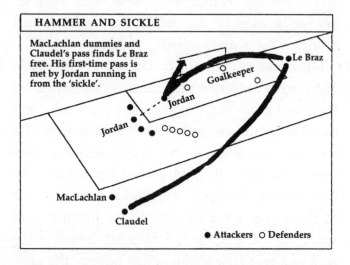

HAMMER AND SICKLE

MacLachlan dummies and Claudel's pass finds Le Braz free. His first-time pass is met by Jordan running in from the 'sickle'.

Le Braz

Goalkeeper

Jordan

Jordan

MacLachlan

Claudel

● Attackers ○ Defenders

As they warmed up for the Highfield match on a clear September evening there appeared to be a new feeling of confidence and understanding in the Sherwood side which had been missing all season.

But one player sitting on the bench wasn't in the best of moods. Thomas always hated it when he was left out of the starting line-up. This was the team sheet for the Highfield game:

'I'm playing well, feeling good. So why have you dropped me?' he'd asked the manager that morning when Joss announced the team.

'Not dropped, lad. You're still young and you're a big asset to the club. I've got to rest you from time to time. Rotate the players a bit.'

'But Pahler's more a centre player.'

'I know, but I want to try him with Franco Jordan inside. Franco needs a big match and he hasn't started too many games. Maybe I'll bring you on in the second half. And then maybe not.'

Typical Joss, thought Thomas. The boss always kept his options open. And he could hardly complain – he'd been keener than anyone to see Joss back in charge of team selection. He knew he couldn't play every game but he was annoyed that he was missing out on the Rovers game. Strikers v Rovers was always the big one in the Headley household, with his little brother being such a big Highfield Rovers fan. Thomas always enjoyed Richie's admiration – it was as if he stood for all Thomas's fans, all the kids who worshipped him, sent him fan mail, named their pet rabbits after him, invited him to their birth-day parties or simply asked for his autograph outside the ground. Richie idolised him and Thomas found it quite hard to tell his brother that he was on the bench for the Premier League clash.

Thomas was joined by the other reserves: Little Mac McEwan, Rory Betts, Ezal Delmonty and Cisco Panto-Gomes. They settled down to watch the game develop. It had rained overnight and the pitch was slippery and fast. There were three bookings in the first 20 minutes, thanks mainly to the conditions rather than any nastiness between the teams. Thomas watched Franco Jordan critically. It was a big leap up from Division One into the top flight, but he had to admit that Franco was pulling his weight in midfield. He was quick and an accurate distributor of the ball, but above all he was very precise in the tackle and held players off when he had possession. Highfield were a class act in midfield and they tested the young player to the full.

With Graham Deek spearheading the attack, Rovers were extremely dangerous on the break and their quick movement across the pitch put the pace of Franco and Petr Pahler to the test. Of the two, the younger player seemed more able to cope than the experienced international.

Then just before half time Drew Stilton scored. It was a classic goal that even Thomas could not fault. Stilton cut in from the left wing to collect a beautifully placed high ball from Big Mac. In a stride he was through the Rovers defence and hit the ball with his supposedly weaker left foot. The Highfield keeper was rooted to the spot and could only watch the ball fly past him. Drew did his inevitable little dance of triumph for the screaming fans. It was a great goal – Ashleigh Coltrane could hardly have executed it better.

At half time Thomas got the nod from Joss to take over from Franco Jordan.

'Keep your cool,' he told the team. 'I'm pleased with your commitment and I've a feeling we're going to get a result today. Keep it tight, especially down the right. They'll push up in the second half and I want Brad to stick closer to young Graham Deek. Jason, you're not getting back from your runs as quickly as you could.'

'Give us a break, Boss,' said Jason. 'That pitch is like a skating rink today.'

'No excuses, lad. You've got a role to play and if you're not punching your weight I've got players on the bench who'll be happy to show you the way.'

Jason grimaced but said nothing. He knew that Joss was right and he respected him for his no-nonsense approach. It was a million miles from the old rubbish they had got used to hearing from PeeWee, Doc and Warren at half time.

Thomas slotted into his usual wide midfield position on the left. Ahead of him Drew was still strutting about, basking in the crowd's appreciation of his first-half goal. Today the Reds were moving as a unit. Thomas experienced that rare and elusive feeling of football being played at the highest level by players who understood each other instinctively. It was wonderful. It was like being part of a great purring engine. He hardly heard the crowd, though the Trent Park roar was back to full volume and almost taking the roof off the stands.

Five minutes from the re-start a solo run by

Claudel tore the Rovers defence apart and his shot almost burst the netting. A minute later Strikers were three up when Drew Stilton ran onto a cross from Jason and headed home off the underside of the bar.

Sherwood Strikers 3   Highfield Rovers 0
Stilton, 40, 46, Claudel, 45

It could easily have been six or seven as the Reds poured forward and the desperate Rovers defence blocked and tackled to keep them out. Then after twenty minutes of their best football of the season Strikers seemed to take their foot off the gas and Highfield began to reassert them-selves in midfield. A foul just outside the area by Psycho Oldie gave Deekie a chance to curl a beautiful free kick round the wall into the top left corner of Sean Pincher's goal.

Then after a goal mouth scramble Deek slotted home his second as he just managed to slide a leg under Sean Pincher's body and squeeze the ball into the net. Three–two: amazingly, Rovers had come back from the dead. The last quarter was an end to end battle. First Drew Stilton hit the post, then Freddy Dade, Thomas's England colleague, put the ball in the net at the other end, but the assistant ref's flag was raised for offside. With eight minutes to go a slip by Dean Oldie let Freddy Dade in again and his 25 yards shot was only parried by Sean Pincher in the Strikers goal. Deek swept in on the rebound to power his shot home for a brilliant hat trick.

It looked as if the Reds would have to settle for a draw and Joss was screaming at them to slow the tempo of the game when Drew Stilton was brought down about ten yards outside the Rovers' area. Drew made a four-course meal of his dive and writhe, though it was just about possible that the Highfield defender had clipped his ankle as he ran past. In spite of the Rovers' protests the ref awarded the foul and Big Mac called for the 'hammer and sickle'. The kick by Claudel found Jason on the run and he curled in a first time centre behind the Rovers' wall. The four players in the 'sickle' were already bearing down on goal and the ball floated over two of them and into the path of Thomas and Petr Pahler. For a second it looked as if they were going to get in each other's way but Thomas rose higher and headed across the goal. He knew he'd timed his header well and as he fell forward he watched the ball elude the diving keeper and drop just under the bar and inside the far post.

Four-three! Strikers were ahead again and somehow the defence held out against the rampant Highfield forwards for the last couple of minutes. A well earned victory at last – and against one of the top teams in the Premier League. Maybe it was a turning point, thought Thomas. The crowd seemed to think so too and they happily chanted one of the old Strikers anthems as the players jogged off the pitch.

'We are the boys in red and white
We love to sing all day and night
We sing a song in harmony
We sing our song of victory.'

9

GOALS FOR ALL

Thomas was none too popular that evening with his little brother.

'Let's face it, a draw would have been a fair result,' protested Richie the Rovers fan. 'The ref should never have given a foul for that dive by Stilton. I feel really sorry for Deekie – scoring a hat trick and finishing on the losing side.'

'Football's like that,' said Thomas, realizing that his brother wouldn't take much comfort from a tired old cliché like that.

'We wuz robbed!' was Richie's reply.

'It was a good game, though,' insisted Thomas.

'I'll give you that,' said Richie grudgingly. 'You took the header well. And I thought Pahler had his best game so far for Strikers.'

Thomas had to agree. He hadn't rated Petr Pahler much at the beginning of the season but he was beginning to get used to the pace of the English game and he was an excellent passer of the ball. There was a good chance that he and Thomas could build up a close partnership in the weeks ahead.

'And another thing,' said Richie. 'Joss Morecombe's gone and pinched the Head-master.'

'The who?'

'The Headmaster' you know, Ronnie Chesters. He runs the Youth school. At least he used to – now he's training rotten Strikers Juniors. I used to rate him but he's a complete traitor.'

Joss had stepped in quickly and hired Ronnie Chesters, England's top youth coach, after Old Doolally had switched back to coaching the first team. That was typical of the boss. He never took his eye off the ball. Even when the first team was in trouble he made sure that the future of the Juniors was in secure hands.

Len Dallal's determination that Joss Morecombe would still be in residence at Strikers after Christmas was soon apparent at training and practice sessions. The first team players had never worked so hard in their lives. Doolally hadn't been ignoring the main squad during his time with the Juniors. He'd watched them play every week and he had pages of notes on each player; lists of strengths and weaknesses to work on, and weekly targets. Thomas found himself working a lot with Paul Claudel and Petr Pahler. Len had noticed that Claudel's instinctive passing was not being instantly read by the two midfielders and he developed a passing structure to increase their understanding and build up a whole series of attacking moves down the left-hand side of the pitch.

It paid off in the derby match away to Danebridge Forest when Paul Claudel went on one of his diagonal runs, beating two players. Pahler peeled off down the wing taking Thomas's marker with him. Instantly Thomas cut inside and ran onto the slotted pass from Claudel. The weight of the pass allowed him to jink past the central defender and fire a curving drive into the corner of the net with his left boot. It was the best goal he'd scored all season.

As the first half wore on the trio of internationals were showing real signs of building up the sort of close understanding which brings terror to opposing defences. Another goal before half time came from a great solo effort by Claudel. He took on three defenders, beat two of them twice and then just as it seemed he had over-run on the far side, he sensed Petr Pahler behind him inside the penalty area. A flicked back-heel turned the entire defence and allowed the Austrian a free shot on goal. He didn't waste his chance, sidestepping the ball wide of the keeper into the net.

Danebridge got one back straight after the interval when a free kick was turned in at the far post by Jon Frohlich. But then the Reds came at them again. This time it was a slick move down the right between Big Mac and Jason Le Braz which ended in a low cross. Little Mac pounced ahead of his defender and drove home. Claudel made it four in the final minute of the game from a set-piece. Strikers lined up for the much talked about 'hammer and sickle' and, seeing a bit of hesitation in the Forest wall, the Frenchman simply went for the double bluff and curled his perfect shot directly round the defenders, just inside the right-hand post and well beyond the grasp of the diving keeper.

The big Frenchman was generous in his praise of the team after the match. 'For the first time I understand that Strikers can be a great team,' he said. 'I have played with many fine stars but Thomas and Petr may be the best players for me. Together we will make the Reds famous across

Europe from Spain to Scandinavia. As famous as the Three Musketeers.'

Joss Morecombe smiled to himself. He couldn't guess what had sparked Claudel into giving his best performance of the season. But now he knew for certain that the French magician was worth every penny he'd paid for him. It was his job now to keep him firing and Joss instinctively saw that young Thomas Headley could play a key part in achieving that.

He decided to share his thoughts with Katie Moncrieff.

'You're as close to Thomas as anyone,' he said to her. 'Tell me what he thinks of Claudel.'

'As a player he rates him as the best in the world,' said Katie. 'He's watched Paul on video for years and he says he's learned a lot from him already this season.'

'And as a person?'

'I don't know. Paul's not an easy person to get close to. We all know he's a bit of a poseur but I'm sure that's a smokescreen. He's suspicious of people because he knows there are a lot of con artists out there trying to take advantage of him. But with Thomas he's different – I think it's a mutual respect thing – although I'd say he was just a bit in awe of Paul.'

'I thought so.'

'Why are you asking me all this?'

Joss smiled. 'Because you're a good friend of Thomas's and you've got his interests at heart. And because, with Paul Claudel alongside him, he could become the greatest player this country's seen for 50 years.'

'So what can I do to help?'

'Well, I was wondering if you'd be interested in writing a couple of big football books.'

'What?'

'I think I can persuade Paul's manager to let you cover his first year with Strikers – that should sell a copy or two. And with a bit of coaxing Elaine Headley might agree to let you loose on Thomas's World Cup diary, or something like that.'

'That would be brilliant,' enthused Katie. Then she gave Joss a quizzical look. 'What are you up to, you old fox? You want me to keep a close eye on the two of them for you, don't you? You're asking me to become a Strikers spy.'

'Spy's a bit strong,' said Joss. 'I see it more as building a friendship. Making people happy.'

'Like I said, you're an old fox, Joss Morecombe.'

'So you'll do it?'

'You arrange it, I'll write the books,' said Katie with a big grin.

On Saturday Strikers returned to Earth after their midweek goal feast. They played a very defensive and negative Border Town in the sort of game which had both sets of fans wondering why they'd bothered to turn up. But just when a 0–0 draw seemed inevitable, Joss Morecombe brought on Franco Jordan and he latched onto a long throw by Dean Oldie and hammered in a volley from fully 25 yards which left the keeper staring in disbelief.

Three wins in a row had taken Sherwood Strikers to a more comfortable half-way position in the league table. A week later they made it four as the team put on a champagne performance in front of the home crowd in serving out a 5–1 thrashing to Derwent Athletic. Claude1 and Stilton got two apiece and Little Mac the fifth. At last Joss Morecombe could start to plan more than one game ahead. For the moment his position was secure and the form of the team seemed to have peaked just in time for the next big test. For on Wednesday the mighty Real Madrid would visit Trent Park. This was the one Joss had been waiting for. Had he put together a team that could make its mark in Europe? Or was it just another false dawn for Strikers? Wednesday night would answer those questions.

Premiership table

	P	W	L	D	F	A	Pts
West Thames Wanderers	12	8	1	3	25	9	27
Barbican	12	6	0	6	24	10	24
Newlynn City	11	7	2	2	25	17	23
Derwent Athletic	12	6	1	5	23	20	23
Highfield Rovers	12	6	3	3	25	18	21
St James	11	6	2	3	19	14	21
Sherwood Strikers	**12**	**5**	**4**	**3**	**22**	**13**	**18**
Danebridge Forest	12	4	2	6	19	18	18
Branston Town	12	4	2	6	17	18	18
Border Town	11	4	3	4	15	15	16
Fenland Rangers	12	4	4	4	17	18	16
Mersey United	11	5	6	0	21	22	15
White Hart United	12	3	4	5	15	16	14
Kingstown Academy	12	3	5	4	18	20	13
Wierdale Harriers	12	2	6	4	18	24	10
Mersey City	11	2	5	4	15	24	10
Southdown United	11	1	4	6	18	23	9
Wednesfield Royals	12	2	7	3	13	21	9
Alexandra Park	12	1	10	1	10	22	4
Wyvern Vale	12	0	9	3	9	26	3

Sherwood Strikers Premiership Analysis

10
THE REAL THING

Real Madrid were a legend, especially to Joss Morecombe who remembered the great team of the fifties, perhaps the greatest team of all time, captained by his own boyhood hero, Di Stefano.

Today's Real Madrid were not quite in that league, but the team had won more European silverware in the past five years than all the English clubs put together. They were formidable opponents, spearheaded by the great Brazilian, Jose Santana, and with a midfield which included Han Krum the Bulgarian captain and the two stars of the Spanish national side, Jaume Serra and Santiago Santa Maria Ruiz.

Joss knew this was the big test of his developing side. Were they ready for it yet? He was missing Dean Oldie and Ashleigh Coltrane, two of his most experienced players in European competition. Psycho was still suspended until the return leg, Ashleigh would be out until January with his break although he hobbled about Trent Park on crutches talking to all the players. There were doubts too about Brad Trainor and Cosimo Lagattello, but they both came through last minute fitness tests. The need to score goals in the home leg finally led Joss towards an attacking formation.

Reserves: Rory Betts, Ezal Delmonty, Sergio Gambolini, Francisco Panto-Gomes, Franco Jordan, Drew Stilton.

Trent Park was bursting with expectant fans. The Strikers supporters – a few louts excepted – were amongst the best Joss Morecombe had come across. They were knowledgeable and committed to their club but never afraid to let the players and management hear the truth. Today there was an air of expectation and pride as they sang the players on to the pitch.

'Here we go, all the way with Strikers,
We're going to give the boys a hand.
So stand up and sing for Strikers,
They're the greatest in the land.'

Joss recalled that only three weeks ago the fans had been in a quite different mood, with:

'We'll score again, don't know where don't
know when,
But I know we'll score again some sunny
day.'

The players' names were announced over the address system and the biggest cheer of the evening so far greeted Paul Claudel and Thomas Headley.

The game began with a flourish. Madrid stormed forward from the whistle and they would have had the ball in the net inside a minute had not Sean Pincher pulled off the most remarkable of saves inside his right post.

Somehow he tipped over a stinging drive with his left hand, but his dive brought him clattering against the upright and he suffered a painful blow to his right shoulder.

Madrid certainly hadn't come to defend. They positioned two players up-field, Santana and the big, angular Di Rivio, and the speed of their midfield was able to open up chance after chance for the forwards to latch onto. After half an hour and several more saves, Pincher had to leave the field with his shoulder injury and Rory Betts replaced him. A minute later he was picking the ball out of his net, beaten by a great boomerang of a shot from Santana from the edge of the penalty area. Rory may have been unsighted but the general view was that he could have made a better effort at reaching the shot. However, a few moments later he made up for it and more, by diving at Santana's feet when the Brazilian was clean through on goal and then somehow getting a leg to Di Rivio's shot from the rebound and deflecting the ball behind for a corner.

Strikers were under the cosh and were lucky not to go three or four goals behind as the brilliant Serra and Santana carved gaping holes in their defence. Rory made two more excellent saves and Big Mac was forced back to man-mark Serra. Before half time Joss had to make another substitution when Tarquin Kelly limped off. He was replaced by Ezal Delmonty who went wide, leaving Ben El Harra to watch over Santana's runs through the centre. It seemed to work and for the first time Strikers began to settle on the ball and the midfield started to make use of the greater possession they were getting.

Thomas went past his marker down the wing and got in a good cross which Little Mac headed only fractionally wide. Then Claudel, who had hardly touched the ball till that moment, broke free of two defenders and delivered a perfect throughball to Thomas who had overlapped with him. Thomas took it down with his knee and shot on the run before the ball had hit the grass. He looked up with dismay to see it cannon off the crossbar and back over his head.

At half time Joss gave them a good report for sticking to the task. 'The work rate's great,' he said. 'Now how about getting back to the game plan? I want to see more movement forwards. You've got pace and fitness. You can force them to defend if you create more space by running off the ball. I want to see Jason attacking down the right more in this half and we need to feed Paul and Thomas on the other wing too. Let's stretch them till they snap. But keep possession.'

Len Dallal had a quiet word with Big Mac and Pasta. He'd noticed that the Madrid offside trap was a bit slow at reacting on clearances. The long ball over the top for Little Mac and Claudel to run onto might catch them on the hop.

Even Doolally couldn't have hoped for more. Pasta's first kick of the second half landed one bounce ahead of Claudel and – wham – his right foot buried it in the back of the net. In spite of the protests of the Real defence, the assistant ref's flag stayed down and the crowd sang its approval.

> 'Like a river flows
> Surely to the sea
> Darling, here's Claudo
> Soon he'll give us three.'

Strikers had now taken control of the game and Real Madrid's incisive attacks became fewer and fewer. The Reds spread the ball, using the full width of the field and the speed of the wide men, Jason down the right and Thomas on the left, was providing plenty of good crosses for Paul

Claudel and Little Mac. Madrid's big defenders, however, were up to the aerial battle; they cleared everything the wide men could throw at them. Something different was needed to break them down.

Joss's response was to bring on Franco Jordan for Little Mac to give Strikers more height and power in the middle. But still the Madrid back line held, and again and again they cleared. From yet another clearance Claudel tackled back and picked up the ball on the halfway line. He found Big Mac out on the wing and took the return pass, going round a defender with his first touch. Thomas saw that a run behind the defence would put him clear, but would Paul pick up his move? Would he slot the pass through before he ran offside? Claudel went round another player and passed just as Thomas was level with the last defender. He was in the clear and onside. The speed of the pass was inch perfect and he ran on to it and fired in a shot a full 20 yards from goal. The curve took it away from the keeper and across the goal and, just as Thomas feared, the angle was too great. It struck the post and rebounded into the path of Claudel who had continued his run. He slammed it into the back of the net. Two-one.

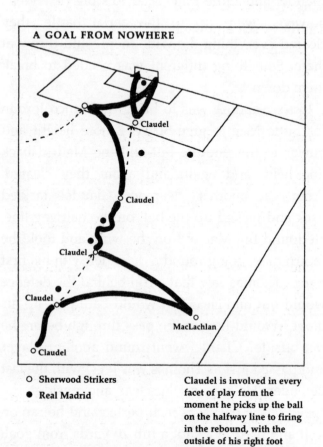

A GOAL FROM NOWHERE

○ Sherwood Strikers
● Real Madrid

Claudel is involved in every facet of play from the moment he picks up the ball on the halfway line to firing in the rebound, with the outside of his right foot

With time running out the Reds were looking for a third. Two–one with the away goal rule would make Madrid favourites in the home leg. Three-one would give Strikers the edge. Paul

Claudel went over and spoke to Big Mac and then they both approached Thomas.

'Get doon the line once ma', Tommeh. But pull tha' cross back tae me. Ya get it?'

For once Thomas had understood – every word. What were Big Mac and the Frenchman planning, he wondered? He didn't have long to think about it – a pass from Pasta found him clear on the left again and he hared down the wing without too much opposition from the Madrid defence. They could mass in the centre and clear his crosses all day, or so they thought. As he reached the by-line Thomas flicked the ball back to Big Mac who was 15 yards in and clear of his marker. The defence came out to meet him and the Strikers skipper immediately dinked a ball over the top of them to Claudel who had run through with Pasta alongside him. Claudel headed down into Cosimo's path and the Sicilian struck the ball with his right foot. He scuffed his shot slightly but the keeper still had no chance and Pasta ran into the goal, picked up the ball, kissed it and saluted the cheers of the crowd.

The entire Strikers team except for Rory packed into the goal with him. The cheers continued as they ran back together in a line to the other end of the pitch. And they were still cheering when the ref blew for the end of the ninety minutes.

Joss walked smiling from the dug-out to congratulate his players. Big Mac was the first to shake his hand. 'Ah ken you'll be stayin' at Trent Park a wee bit longer tha' noo, Gaffer,' he said with a smile.

'I imagine they'll keep me on for another week or two,' said Joss.

'They'd be daft as a ha'penny watch tae let tha goo tha noo. And the supporters are no fur havin' it.'

'It's good to be on a winning streak, Mac,' said Joss. 'Football's a funny game and you have to learn to enjoy the good times.' But for all his caginess the boss had a gleam in his eye which said: this is the team I've dreamed of managing all my life. And before long it's going to be up with the greats.

Results

Highfield Rovers 2 – Sherwood Strikers 0
    (Charity Shield)
St James 3 – Sherwood Strikers 1
West Thames Wanderers 1 – Sherwood Strikers 0
Sherwood Strikers 1 – Weirdale Harriers 1

Galatasaray 2 – Sherwood Strikers 0
    (UEFA Cup)
Barbican 2 – Sherwood Strikers 2
Sherwood Strikers 1 – Southdown United 0
Sherwood Strikers 3 – Galatasaray 0
    (UEFA Cup)
Wednesfield Royals 2 – Sherwood Strikers 1
Newlynn City 3 – Sherwood Strikers 1
Sherwood Strikers 1 – Fenland Rangers 1
Sherwood Strikers 4 – Highfield Rovers 3
Danebridge Forest 1 – Sherwood Strikers 4
Sherwood Strikers 1 – Branston Town 0
Sherwood Strikers 5 – Derwent Athletic 1
Sherwood Strikers 3 – Real Madrid 1
    (UEFA Cup)